THE LAST OF THE JEDI

THE LAST OF THE JEDI

DARK WARNING

BY JUDE WATSON

SCHOLASTIC INC.
New York   Toronto   London   Auckland   Sydney
Mexico City   New Delhi   Hong Kong   Buenos Aires

www.starwars.com
www.scholastic.com

ISBN 0-439-68135-9

Cover art by John Van Fleet

12 11 10 9 8 7 6 5 4 3 2 1   5 6 7 8 9 10/0

Printed in the U.S.A.
First printing, September 2005

CHAPTER ONE

He was getting closer. Within minutes, he would spot them.

Obi-Wan Kenobi watched from the cockpit of a grounded, dilapidated cruiser as Boba Fett methodically searched the crowded Red Twins spaceport, looking for his prey. The Jedi saw Fett's compact body move down the rows of space cruisers, his helmet turning as he and his surveillance devices took everything in.

Obi-Wan could see that Fett was moving in a pattern that only seemed random. The bounty hunter was cutting over after every third ship to the next line, then skipping a row, moving backward, then moving forward on alternate rows. It was a complex pattern to follow for an ordinary being, but not for an exceptional tracker like Boba Fett . . . or a Jedi like Obi-Wan. To an observer, Fett would seem to be ambling in a casual fashion, but within a few minutes he would have checked out every ship in the spaceport. Including the Jedi's.

Obi-Wan saw his companion, Ferus Olin, watching Fett from the shadows of the cockpit.

"I give us three minutes," Ferus said.

"Two and a half," Obi-Wan amended.

Ferus and Obi-Wan had landed at the Red Twin spaceport just a few minutes before, along with their stowaway, thirteen-year-old Trever Flume. They had tangled with Boba Fett on the planet Bellassa, and were acutely aware of his skills. Plus, he had another bounty hunter with him — D'harhan, a cyborg with an unattractive but lethal laser cannon for a head. Imperial security forces, led by the Inquisitor Malorum, had hired the bounty hunters to catch Ferus, a hero of the resistance movement on Bellassa.

Even as Obi-Wan ticked off their possibilities for escape, he wanted to kick himself down the spaceport for being here in the first place. He had been on Tatooine when he had heard Ferus was in trouble — Tatooine, where he was supposed to stay and watch over the young Luke Skywalker. Obi-Wan had always liked the former Jedi apprentice, who had left the Order right before he was scheduled to take the Trials — in fact, he had been relieved that someone who had been so close to the Jedi was still alive. But was saving Ferus enough of a reason to risk leaving Tatooine? Obi-Wan had been racked with indecision . . . until he heard his former Master, Qui-Gon Jinn, who had at last spoken to him, thanks to Qui-Gon's training with the Whills.

What a shock it had been to hear Qui-Gon's voice, and how unsurprising it should have been that Qui-Gon had been the one to tell him to leave. Things much bigger than Ferus were at stake, and Qui-Gon told him he needed to follow the Living Force . . . and his feelings.

So he had followed them to Bellassa, had become tangled up with the resistance, and had barely escaped with Ferus. Now he was halfway across the galaxy from Tatooine, with two bounty hunters on his tail. Meanwhile, Inquisitor Malorum was getting closer to the truth of Luke and Leia's existence, by investigating Polis Massa, the place where their mother, Padmé Amidala, had died. Obi-Wan knew he had to stop Malorum . . . but first he had to dodge the bounty hunters on his trail. Obi-Wan couldn't return to Tatooine until he had shaken them off. He couldn't lead anyone to the hidden son of Anakin Skywalker.

"Hey, fellas?" Trever spoke up. His spiky blue hair seemed to quiver with anxiety as he looked from Obi-Wan to Ferus. "Not to jump in here, but shouldn't we be taking off in a hurry-up-and-blast-me-outta-here sort of way?"

"He'll just follow us," Ferus said. "And there's no way we'll shake him in this bucket. We need a different ship. This won't end until we get one and get out of here."

"Right, excellent," Trever said. "Not a problem. Just give me a minute."

"You can't steal one," Obi-Wan warned.

"Sure I can," the young teenager said. "All I have to do is bypass the initial ignition security controls, then —"

Obi-Wan held up his hand. "*Then* we'll have security to contend with as well as Boba Fett. We have to do this without causing any alarm."

"There's a new concept for you, kid," Ferus said to Trever.

"I'll try to keep up," Trever replied with a grin. Despite his young age, he had been the most adept street thief in the capital city of Ussa on Bellassa. At only thirteen, he had controlled a large portion of the black market. When things got too hot for him, he had stowed away with Obi-Wan and Ferus as they'd made their escape.

But if things had been one-sun hot then, they were three-sun hot now.

Quickly, Obi-Wan, Ferus, and Trever gathered their survival packs and jumped off the ship. Obi-Wan made sure to cloak himself, his head unrecognizable under a hood. He did not want to be recognized by Boba Fett.

"We'll have to try a trade. The trick is," Obi-Wan

said under his breath as he kept his eyes on the roving figure of Boba Fett, "to pick the right ship. And the right pilot. He's got to think he's getting a deal, but the deal can't be too good or he'll get suspicious."

"I wonder where D'harhan is," Ferus said.

"Probably stayed on the ship," Obi-Wan guessed. "He'd attract the attention of security."

They disembarked from their ship and threaded through the grumbling crowd. The new Empire regulations had made check-in slow, and departures were often held up while lengthy security checks were gone through. Pilots and passengers milled around, killing time until their numbers flashed on a huge screen overhead. At that point they joined the line to the security checkpoint inside the main building. Some of them had turned the area in front of the hangar into an informal picnic area, and the bartering of food and drink was going on in a lively exchange typical of pilots, as they variously insulted and flattered each other into trades.

Obi-Wan perused the ships. They needed something with a hyperdrive, something spaceworthy but not too flashy. They needed speed and some kind of weaponry. Knowing Boba Fett's heavily armed Firespray attack ship, laser cannons would certainly come in handy.

In his head, Obi-Wan counted off the rows of

ships and the complex pattern Fett was following. If they kept weaving in a counter-pattern, they wouldn't run into him. Of course, he would find their ship very soon, and his surveillance would intensify. But if they were lucky, they'd blast off the spaceport by then.

If they were lucky.

Which they weren't.

Boba Fett changed his pattern and spotted them from afar, attacking immediately from behind. The Force surged, warning Obi-Wan only a split second before the bounty hunter was on them.

Blaster bolts streaked toward them. Obi-Wan leaped and dodged. He didn't want to use his lightsaber — not here, with a crowd looking on. News that a Jedi had been seen would spread, and the hunt would intensify. As far as the galaxy was concerned, all the Jedi had been wiped out. Any Jedi who was found would quickly share the same fate.

Ferus's Jedi training made him move quicker than an ordinary bystander, dodging almost in time with Obi-Wan. Trever's street smarts sent him diving under the belly of a ship. A surprised pilot poked his head out of his cockpit dome a second after blaster bolts ripped into his hull. He started to swear at Boba Fett, but backed down when Fett swiveled and aimed his Westar-34 blaster in his direction.

The diversion gave Obi-Wan two seconds — two

seconds that spun out into a long moment of contemplation, as he pinpointed the exact location of the ships surrounding him, the crowd, the buildings. He saw opportunity for temporary shelter but he did not see what he was looking for — an avenue of escape.

When in doubt, he thought, *do the unexpected.*

Obi-Wan charged, his hood still concealing his identity. He lunged into the teeth of the blaster fire, weaponless. A surprised Boba Fett took a step back. He was too good to stumble, but for the smallest whisper of a second he was slightly off balance. Obi-Wan saw it. Fett's left side was the vulnerable point.

He leaped. In midair, he twisted, coming down with one boot planted squarely on Boba Fett's left knee. But to his surprise, Fett didn't go over. Obi-Wan felt the bounty hunter's body give, but suddenly Fett reversed direction, planting himself more firmly. Obi-Wan was stopped cold and had the unpleasant sensation of feeling an armored elbow smash into the back of his head, sending him to the ground.

He'd seen that move before. The memory of a desperate fight on Kamino came back to him. Jango Fett had taught his son well. If only Obi-Wan had remembered it in time.

Ferus came charging as Obi-Wan rolled to his feet, ducking blaster bolts with his Jedi reflexes.

Suddenly, the ship next to them exploded. Obi-Wan and Ferus were sent flying by the power of the blast, riding a cushion of air that slammed them into the permacrete. Molten durasteel rained around them. Ferus ducked as a cockpit seat landed only millimeters from his head.

"Well, hello, D'harhan," Ferus said through gritted teeth.

There was a moment of shocked silence after the blast, and then sirens began to sound. Pilots and passengers searched for a safe vantage point from which to watch the battle. It had been a boring afternoon, and no one minded a little diversion. It promised to be a good fight.

Ferus popped to his feet. His face was black with smoke and dust from the explosion. "Love the way those guys introduce themselves," he said to Obi-Wan.

Boba Fett was taking advantage of the explosion to move in, his blaster bolts streaking through the air. Obi-Wan knew he had to get under cover, away from the spectators. Somewhere he could use his lightsaber without attracting attention.

"Go left," he said tersely to Ferus. "Keep D'harhan occupied."

"Why do *I* always get the mean guy?" Ferus replied, with more humor than Obi-Wan remembered him having as an apprentice.

Ferus seemed to float away, he moved so gracefully, sliding between two starships and disappearing. Obi-Wan used the Force to propel his jump, clearing the ship on his right and landing on the peaked durasteel roof of the hangar. There was a dormer midway down the roof, a window that was built into the roof itself. Obi-Wan dived for cover behind the overhang.

Fett was wearing a jetpack, and he soared above to land on the roof only seconds after Obi-Wan. He advanced cautiously, unable to see the Jedi. Obi-Wan activated his lightsaber. He did it so rarely now that he felt a surge of feelings flood him when he did, something close to pain and joy, a remembrance of what it had once meant to be a Jedi. Once he had traveled freely through the galaxy. Now he had to hide what he was. Now all he knew was secrecy and caution.

Blaster bolts suddenly ripped through the dormer, only centimeters from where he waited. Boba Fett was taking no chances.

Obi-Wan didn't move, even though he felt the sear of heat on his cheek.

He heard the footsteps approaching. Just as they reached the corner of the dormer, just when there was only a split second before Fett would see him, Obi-Wan leaped out.

But Fett must have been expecting this. Taking

barely a second to aim, he fired the concussion missile in his jetpack.

Obi-Wan felt the shock waves reverberate. He was blown off the roof, his body lifting into the air like a scrap of cloth. He slowed down the moment, looking for a way to land that wouldn't involve smashing into the permacrete rising toward him.

He reached for the grapnel line on his utility belt. He sent it flying as he fell, the hook catching on the edge of the roof. He bounced in the air, hard, wrenching his shoulder as he quickly swung himself back up. He hit the roof and kept going, charging at Fett, his lightsaber glowing. He severed Fett's blaster rifle in one clean stroke.

Obi-Wan had nowhere to go as Fett suddenly slammed into him, wrapping his arms around the Jedi's body, knocking away his lightsaber, and propelling him backward, trying to push him off the roof. Instead of trying to break Fett's grip, Obi-Wan seized his arms, and the two men shot off the edge, spinning in midair. The crowd below saw them now and gasped.

The two bodies fell through the air for several long seconds before Fett activated his jetpack. As he fired his thrusters, he maneuvered the jetpack so he could slam Obi-Wan against the side of the building repeatedly. Obi-Wan felt the blows shudder through his bones.

Fett reversed and came at the building again. Obi-Wan saw the solid duracrete zooming toward his face. He called on the Force to help. He would need it. At the last moment, he drew his legs up and kicked out. The jolt radiated up through his skull. They spun out, and Obi-Wan used the opportunity to loosen Fett's hold. He dropped, gathering the Force to ease his landing and recapture his fallen lightsaber.

He didn't injure himself, but the pain that traveled up his legs told him that his push off the wall had cost him. Spectators scattered as he rose to his feet. Boba Fett was coming after him, relentless.

Ferus ran through the crowd. Obi-Wan felt the Force surge in warning as another cannon blast from D'harhan leveled part of the hangar.

Ferus was blown back by the blast. D'harhan kept coming. Boba Fett was gathering himself for another assault. Obi-Wan charged forward, grabbed Ferus, and pulled him to his feet.

"Come on," Obi-Wan urged. He hadn't come this far to lose Ferus now.

He helped Ferus stumble past the rubble and leap into the half-demolished hangar. Massive doors were on the other end, firmly shut tight. D'harhan and Boba Fett followed through the opening, blocking any way out.

Obi-Wan and Ferus were trapped.

CHAPTER TWO·

Fett and D'harhan didn't give them a chance to form a strategy. The bounty hunters were all movement, D'harhan passing Fett a blaster so they could both fire at will. The air filled with debris and smoke.

"I wish I had a lightsaber," Ferus muttered as he and Obi-Wan dived for cover behind a large ship awaiting repair. He had turned in his lightsaber when he'd left the Order. "Now would be an excellent time to draw yours, Obi-Wan."

Still, Obi-Wan waited. He and Ferus settled back against a large repair console filled with tools. He saw the smoke curl from D'harhan's head, and he knew the laser cannons had overheated. Boba Fett's blaster fire couldn't penetrate the ship. They were safe for the moment.

But only for the moment. Obi-Wan scanned the hangar. Despite D'harhan's incredible firepower, he knew Fett was the greater threat. Of the two of them, Fett had the cunning.

Above, struts held the roof in place. A series of arcing flexible durasteel supports crisscrossed the high space. Half of the roof had been blasted off when Fett had fired the concussion missile.

The support arches would be an excellent place to stage a battle. Fett had his jetpack, but D'harhan would be at a disadvantage. He would have to remain on the ground.

Obi-Wan pointed with his chin. "Can you make it?" he asked Ferus, indicating the gridwork above.

Ferus grinned. "Can a bantha fly?"

"Actually, no."

"You're such a stickler for details, Obi-Wan."

Suddenly, the Force surged, and Obi-Wan heard a slight whine. D'harhan had released another blast from his laser cannon. The cruiser under repair suffered a direct hit. Flames blew back toward Obi-Wan and Ferus, and they leaped to avoid them.

It was just what Boba Fett was waiting for. Obi-Wan's lightsaber danced, deflecting the bounty hunter's blaster fire as Obi-Wan leaped to safety on a strut high above. Ferus landed on a ship next to the now-destroyed cruiser, then used the momentum of his jump to make a second leap, calling on the Force this time. He sailed into the air, his fingertips grazing the lowermost beam. Obi-Wan saw panic in his eyes. He reached down and grabbed Ferus's wrist, then hauled him up.

Boba Fett moved quickly, activating the propellants on his jetpack and zooming into the air, firing as he came. Deflecting the bolts, Obi-Wan took up the rear as he and Ferus raced to the roof opening.

Ferus had his own crude weaponry to employ. He reached into his pocket, then tossed something at Fett, a shining disk that spun in a clean line, straight toward him. Fett dodged, but the disk hit his armor near the shoulder, searing a crack into the surface. Obi-Wan realized that Ferus had filled his pockets with the round laser cutting blades that fit into a servocutter tool. He tossed another and another, and Fett had a hard time dodging them. With every burst from his jetpack, he zoomed perilously close to the beams.

Silently congratulating Ferus for his inventiveness, Obi-Wan reversed course and charged toward the careening Fett, swinging his lightsaber over his head as he ran. He pinpointed the bolts that held the sheets of durasteel in place for the roof, hitting each one with a quick, cutting touch in a careful pattern. Now all D'harhan had to do was cooperate.

The cyborg was nothing if not predictable. Obi-Wan saw his laser cannon revolve as it followed him. The red tracking light began to pulse.

Boba Fett instantly knew what was going to happen. Obi-Wan saw a new urgency in his attempts to dodge Ferus's spinning laser cuttings as he dove down to stop D'harhan.

He was too late. The cannonfire streaked toward them. Obi-Wan had anticipated it and swung on a beam, flying through the air toward the rear of the hangar. Ferus was close on his heels.

The firepower ripped into the roof where Obi-Wan had been. The bolts had all been cut by the lightsaber on this particular panel, and the thin durasteel peeled back like the rind of a fruit, falling toward the floor below.

Boba Fett made it to safety, but D'harhan was caught. The falling durasteel panel hit him squarely on the back, crashing him to the ground and pinning his legs.

Obi-Wan and Ferus dropped to the floor below. Swinging his lightsaber, Obi-Wan advanced on Fett. Ferus took shelter behind the various ships, trying to get behind Boba Fett so they could corner him. With D'harhan temporarily out of commission, this would be their best chance to stop Fett.

Unfortunately the damage had not gone unnoticed by the spaceport security. A fight among pilots was one thing, property damage another. Suddenly speeders soared into the space, piloted by security officers armed with blaster rifles. Fett was their first target, and they headed for him. The bounty hunter now had his hands full as he turned to meet their assault.

With a quick swipe, Obi-Wan destroyed the control panel on D'harhan's laser cannon. The cyborg's usual smile was now a grimace. His expressionless voice was hoarse. "You think you've won, don't you. But we don't lose. One day you'll be another Jedi prisoner on Coruscant. Malorum has his ways."

Blaster fire suddenly ripped into the ground next to them. More security officers had arrived.

"Don't move," an amplified voice said.

As Ferus joined them, D'harhan's grin grew wider. "Now we'll all be in prison together."

Ferus leaned down. "We're not going anywhere with you, you slab of circuit parts."

Obi-Wan heard the hum of an engine. He saw through the partially open door that a space cruiser had jockeyed out of the line and was edging toward the hangar.

Trever.

Ferus saw him, too. "Time to catch the air taxi," he said.

They raced toward the ship. Trever spun it around and released the landing ramp even as he began to rise in the air. With a flying leap, Obi-Wan and Ferus hit the ramp and pulled themselves onboard.

Blaster bolts peppered the closing ramp as they

ran up into the belly of the ship. They reached the cockpit just as Trever sent the cruiser screaming above the spaceport.

As they streaked up into the atmosphere, the Red Twins dwindled into two pulsating crimson dots, then just a single reddish glow.

"Nice driving, kid," Ferus told Trever. "Where'd you get the ship?"

Trever's face was flushed. "Traded for it while you were dancing around. I figured we'd need a clean getaway."

"Not so clean," Obi-Wan said. A glowing light was streaking across the sky.

Boba Fett had escaped to his ship.

CHAPTER THREE

Trever looked at the control panel. "Aw, you've got to be kidding me. This guy is really starting to get on my nerves."

Without taking his eyes from the fighter following them, Obi-Wan said, "We can lose him in hyperspace."

"Right," Trever said. "If only we had a hyperdrive."

Ferus rotated and fixed Trever with an incredulous look. "You didn't trade for a ship with a hyperdrive?"

"I didn't have much time, you know," Trever protested.

"We're at the edge of the Outer Rim," Ferus said. "Every ship has a hyperdrive out here. Except the one we're on."

"I didn't see you being choosy when I came to rescue you," Trever shot back.

"If you two don't mind a suggestion," Obi-Wan said. "The what-ifs aren't helping. Fett is gaining."

Ferus was starting to hate it when Obi-Wan was right. "You want me to take over?" he asked, pointing to the controls.

"Sure." Obi-Wan crossed to the nav computer. "I hate flying. And, Trever, I think this might be a little beyond your experience."

Ferus took over the controls. He wondered about his own experience. For the past few years he'd been living quietly on Bellassa, trying to put his Jedi past behind him. The decision to leave had been the hardest one he'd ever made, and it had haunted him every day and every night. He'd let his rival, Anakin Skywalker, push him into leaving. He'd left behind a life of missions and meaning for . . . isolation. He and his friend Roan had lived quietly — until the rise of the Empire had turned them into Rebels. Ferus had found his cause once more. And he had vowed to stick to it this time, until the Empire was defeated. Roan was lost now, Bellassa a new part of his past. Once more, Ferus found himself on the path of a Jedi — but unsure whether it was a path he was allowed to take.

He pushed the speed, then dropped back, trying to get a feel for the unfamiliar engines. "I'm just going to have to outfly him."

Obi-Wan cast an uneasy glance out the cockpit window. "I have confidence in your piloting skills,

Ferus, but I've seen this Firespray in action. For a small ship, it's impressive. Don't let it fool you. In addition to those blaster cannons, it has laser cannons and seismic minelayers."

"Piece of sweetcake," Trever said, but he looked pale as he saw how quickly Fett was gaining on them. "Don't you want to speed up?" he asked Ferus nervously.

"We know he can outrun us," Ferus pointed out. "The only way we're going to win this is if we're able to outmaneuver him."

Obi-Wan studied the star map. "Let me see if I can find an asteroid shower to hide in or a dense nebula," Obi-Wan said. "We need to play hide-and-seek."

They were almost within firing distance now. Obi-Wan quickly flipped through the different quadrants on the nav computer. "There's a dense nebula close by. All uninhabited star clusters. If we can manage to hold on, we can make it in a few minutes."

The armored plating on Boba Fett's ship slid back and the laser cannon sprang to life. Streaks of light headed toward them. Ferus went into a steep dive even as Fett put on speed, zooming toward them.

"I didn't think he'd be . . . quite this fast," Ferus said, pushing the speed and making a hard right.

The cannonfire just missed them. Another barrage flew in their direction.

Ferus tumbled and turned the ship, spinning and diving. Trever was slammed against the console and quickly leaped into a seat in order to grab the armrests.

They were in a race now, a race they couldn't possibly win. The attack sent shock waves that buffeted the ship, rocking it. It shook so hard that Obi-Wan was afraid it would break apart. He felt his teeth rattle.

"We'd better get there soon," Ferus said. "We're running out of fuel."

"He said he'd just refilled it!" Trever protested.

"Never trust a pilot, kid," Ferus said.

The cannon fired again, and though Ferus went into a dive, the ship quaked as it was struck. Fett followed up the cannonfire with a targeting torpedo.

"Hang on!" Ferus shouted.

The ship dived, then looped up. The torpedo followed, tracking them precisely.

"This is a cargo ship, right?" Obi-Wan asked Trever. The boy nodded. "Release the cargo."

Trever flipped the switch. The cargo bay opened and spilled out empty bins and boxes. At the same moment, Ferus pushed the ship into another steep dive. The torpedo's tracking device followed the cargo instead.

"That'll only work once," Ferus said. "And we've got a problem. I don't think the power systems are used to getting knocked around like this. We have some yellow warning lights flashing. Our systems are failing."

"Nebulae coming up!" Trever shouted.

It wasn't a moment too soon. Ferus counted off the seconds as Fett pounded behind them. The Force filled the cabin. In times of need, Ferus was able to access it and use it — that had never fully gone away. He felt it move through him, and he relaxed his grip on the controls. Once, he had based his life on trusting the Force. He had to remember to do that again.

The ship suddenly entered a tunnel of tiny stars rotating around a central energy core. Golden light filled the ship, and the atmospheric disturbance caused it to bounce alarmingly. "Hang on!" Ferus shouted. He maneuvered the cruiser so that it rode the currents, rotating as it jolted from one edge of the star corridor to the other. "How long will we be in this?" he barked to Obi-Wan.

"Not long. We're on the edge of an unstable current, but it's moving fast away from us."

Fett followed, not giving up, just as intrepid as Ferus — and just as willing to push his ship.

Obi-Wan hung on to the console as he studied the star map. There was incomplete information here, gaps in the mapping, no doubt because of the volatility of the atmosphere. "It looks like there's a planet called Deneter up ahead. It was abandoned after the Clone Wars — it was so decimated by battles that the population emigrated to the Core. It has twenty orbiting uninhabited satellites." He shouted out the coordinates to Ferus. They might be able to lose Fett among the satellites.

They passed through the star tunnel and into the planet's atmosphere. Ferus pushed the ship, zooming from one satellite to another, lurking behind one to zoom out behind the next. Boba Fett stayed on their tail, blasting his cannons.

"This isn't working," Obi-Wan said. "We can't shake him."

"I'm not out of tricks yet," Ferus muttered, hoping it was true. "Trever, remember your gravsled action?"

On the streets of Ussa, Trever had used the unwieldy gravsled like an airspeeder, pushing its capabilities in order to evade Empire security. "Which action?" Trever asked, his eyes on Fett's ship.

"The one where you pretend to spin out, and then recover and zoom off?" Ferus said.

"Yeah. Worked every time."

"How'd you do it?"

"Well, it takes a certain touch," Trever said. "And an extra boost on the stabilizers."

"I'll need a boost from another system," Ferus said. "Can you patch in some power from the hydraulics?"

"Wait a second," Obi-Wan said. "That could leave us without enough braking power to land."

Another barrage of cannonfire sent the ship into a steep dive. This time, the blast hit them in the rear. The ship careened out of control for several long, agonizing seconds while Ferus fought to stabilize. At last, with a great groan, the ship righted itself.

"Then again," Obi-Wan said, "we can worry about landing when the time comes."

"My thoughts exactly," Ferus said through gritted teeth.

Trever dived to the floor and wrenched open the engine panel. He leaped inside the small space. "I don't have much experience with sublight engines, but . . ." They heard muttering and clanking. "Got it!" Trever shouted from below.

"Okay, everyone," Ferus said. "When I say 'hang on,' I really mean it this time."

Ferus speeded up, pushing the engines past maximum now. A slight wobble on the wings told them the ship was at the edge of its control. "Here we go," he muttered. The ship began to list, as though he'd lost control of the left engine. Dizzily, it spun, falling now through space, straight toward the asteroid. Fett followed, no doubt to record their death spiral . . . and hasten their end. Laser cannons streaked their firepower through the atmosphere, but they were traveling too erratically for any of the targeting computers to get a fix on them.

The surface of the satellite loomed. At the last moment, Ferus pulled the ship out, its control centers screaming with the effort. Fett zoomed past them. Now *he* was the one fighting for control. They watched as his ship careened close to the surface. Fett had no choice but to crash-land.

There was a small bloom of fire, and they saw smoke rise.

Obi-Wan studied the life-form sensor. "He's evacuated the ship. It's not destroyed, but its not going anywhere soon."

Ferus soared back up into the atmosphere. "I hope that's the last we see of him," he said. "But somehow I don't think so. Now, I'm afraid, we have our own landing problem to deal with."

CHAPTER FOUR

They didn't have many choices. They could land on the uninhabited planet, but they'd be a little too close to Boba Fett for comfort. Besides, they had no reason to think they'd be able to scavenge fuel to get back off.

"We've got one chance," Obi-Wan said as he scanned the nav computer. "The computer is showing we don't have enough fuel to make it, but we might be able to eke out a few more kilometers than the computer shows. It's a fairly large planet; so there's bound to be an orbit dock or an orbiting shipyard. It's called Acherin."

"Sounds familiar," Ferus said.

"It was where one of the last sieges of the Clone Wars took place," Obi-Wan said briefly. The name of the planet brought a heavy load to his heart. His friend Garen Muln had been Commander of the Republic forces on Acherin — and had presumably died there on that awful day when the clone troopers had turned against the Jedi, slaughtering their former generals on the order of the Sith Lord who was now Emperor.

"Plug in the coordinates," Ferus said. "It's our only shot."

There was nothing to do now but hope that the fuel would hold out. As they spun through space, they tried not to tick off the kilometers in their heads. Finally, they approached the planet, a violet-tinged haze in the distance.

Obi-Wan worked the comm unit, trying to raise a response. "This is strange," he said. "I can't get an answer. Not only that, but there's no chatter on the open lines."

"That *is* strange," Ferus said. "Keep trying. Is there some kind of atmospheric disturbance in the air?"

"No. They have a dense inner atmosphere, but nothing that should block communications."

"We're going to have to enter their atmosphere," Ferus said. "I hate to enter anyplace without permission these days, but we have no choice."

He pulled back on speed as they approached Acherin.

"What's that?" Trever asked, pointing to some orange streaks in the sky.

"Could be some naturally occurring cosmic gas," Obi-Wan said.

"But we're in the inner atmosphere," Trever said.

Ferus immediately started turning the ship. "In certain conditions, like a dense atmosphere, the afterburn of a missile can leave —"

A sudden streak crossed the sky. This time, they knew exactly what it was.

"That's cannonfire," Obi-Wan said. "But what —"

Suddenly, an imposing fleet of assault ships appeared, heading directly toward them.

"The Empire," Trever said.

Fighters took off from one of the assault ships — chasing a trio of small starfighters that now shot across the sky. The Imperial fighters began to chase the three renegades.

Ferus swallowed. "Great. Out of all the planets in the galaxy, we have to pick one in the middle of a war."

"We're going to have to land," Obi-Wan said. He quickly accessed the surface mapping systems. "Just put it down — we're nowhere near a spaceport, and we don't want to blunder into the Empire's hands anyway."

Quickly Obi-Wan scanned the topographical sensors. "There's an area below in a canyon that would give us plenty of cover." He gave Ferus the coordinates.

Suddenly, one of the renegade starfighters peeled off from the others. It bore down on them, flying so close its belly almost scraped the roof of their craft.

"It's forcing me down!" Ferus shouted. "What's going on?"

"And it's drawing fire," Obi-Wan added. "It's alerted the Empire to our position."

"Yeah, this just keeps getting better."

They screamed down through the sky. The surface of the planet loomed.

"I can't hold this course," Ferus said.

Cannonfire shook the ship.

The ship on top of them was hit. Smoke suddenly obscured their vision.

"We're going to crash-land!" Ferus shouted, wrestling with the controls.

With a horrible groaning sound, the ship hit ground and skidded on rock. Ferus controlled the landing, but the battering it received from the rocks took its toll. It came to rest on one side, metal screaming against the rough ground.

They activated the landing ramp, which only opened partway. Ferus searched the pilot's compartment and found an old blaster, which he held in his hand as he led the way out.

A short distance away, the pilot of the renegade

starfighter had emerged from its canopy — with a blaster at the ready.

Blaster fire streaked toward them, trying to pin them in one small area.

"Don't move!" the pilot shouted. "If you move, you're dead."

CHAPTER FIVE

The helmeted pilot stood on the hull of the ship, casually balanced, with both hands on the blaster. Obi-Wan reached out a hand and Force-pushed. The pilot stumbled back . . . as Ferus raised his own blaster and Obi-Wan leaped forward to place the blade of his lightsaber above the pilot's neck.

The pilot looked up with wide, dark blue eyes.

"Well," she said, "what do you know. A Jedi."

"Who are you?" Obi-Wan asked.

"Raina Quill. I'm a commander in the Acherin resistance. Pleased to make your acquaintance. That is, if you could manage to take your lightsaber off my neck."

She was a humanoid woman of about Ferus's age. Her gaze seemed friendly, if intense, but Obi-Wan wasn't about to let her free yet.

"Why did you force us down?"

"Because you were about to land in the middle

of enemy-controlled territory, right within range of a turbolaser. I had a feeling you wouldn't like that. Hey, I thought all the Jedi were dead."

Obi-Wan deactivated his lightsaber. "Not all."

"Apparently." She gingerly came to a sitting position. "Ow. As it is, we're still behind enemy lines. And I have a feeling those starfighters didn't lose us. They had better things to do. But I bet they broadcast our landing site to the ground army."

"Who's the enemy?" Ferus asked.

"The Empire, of course," she said.

"But you were a Separatist planet."

Raina rose to her feet and took off her helmet, shaking out a long auburn braid. "That doesn't mean we support the Empire. We wanted the right to secede from the Republic, not to turn the galaxy into a place of absolute power. Now we've got an Emperor breathing down our necks. Anyway, we were negotiating a truce with the Republic army when the Clone Wars ended. After we got a look at the Empire, we decided to call off the truce and keep fighting instead."

"So how's it going?" Trever asked.

"We've been fighting for almost a year," she said. "They thought they'd crush us in a matter of weeks. But they can't let us win. We know that. We're making a last stand in our ancient city of Eluthan. We've got our army concentrated there. It's a walled city, and we've evacuated most of the civilians. We should try to get there as quickly as we can. And," she added with a rueful glance at their ships, "I'm afraid we have to walk."

"Did you know the Commander of the Republic Forces?" Obi-Wan asked her.

"Garen Muln? Yes, I met him once, when we were negotiating the truce. But you should talk to our commander, Toma. He dealt with Muln. He was with him on that last day . . . the day the Chancellor said that all Jedi were enemies."

The day of the slaughter. Obi-Wan felt Ferus glance at him. Ferus knew Garen had been Obi-Wan's good friend. Ferus had met him as an apprentice, in what he still thought of as his previous life.

"Look, we'd better get to Eluthan," Raina continued. "You can talk to Toma there."

Obi-Wan and Ferus exchanged a glance. They really didn't have any choice. They needed a ship to get off-planet, and Raina was their best bet to find one.

They looked at Trever, and he shrugged. "I guess I'm along for the ride."

"We'd better get going," Raina urged.

They followed her through the canyon into a dense wood. "Much of Acherin is open land," she told them. "We only have three cities. Eluthan is the center of our culture. We fortified it heavily during the Clone Wars and we have a shield operating. That's why we've retreated there."

They walked quickly for several kilometers. Ferus tossed a pack of protein pellets to Trever. He could see that the boy was tiring.

"We only have a few kilometers to go," Raina said in a low tone. "The Empire has ringed the outskirts of the city with their army. We might run into some droid scouts. With any luck we can slip through. I know some shortcuts."

They picked up their pace, close to running now. They came to a vast open field studded with massive standing stones, some of them hundreds of meters high. In the distance, a walled city loomed. It was built on a plateau, and the thick stone walls rose against a bleak yellow sky. It had been designed for fortification, but it was clear that the makers had an eye for beauty, too. The stone was laid in a pattern, and the contrasting grays and dark blues seemed to make up a sculpture of weathered stone and deep colors. There was a grandeur about it that made Obi-Wan and Ferus stop in their tracks.

Raina noticed their reaction. "It is our treasure," she said simply. "And we believe it will protect us from anything."

Not the Empire, Obi-Wan thought.

Suddenly a high whine cut through the air.

"It's a compact assault vehicle," Raina said. "Follow me."

They ran behind her to enter a dense area of the standing stones. They stood, their backs to the stone, while the CAV approached, a droid piloting it.

Obi-Wan knew the vehicles. They were small and agile, but prone to sensor jamming. He assumed that the Empire was using them primarily for surveillance in this area. One droid could cover a great deal of territory, and the vehicle was equipped with a medium-sized blaster cannon.

The CAV sped past.

"There'll be more," Raina said.

They moved on. They went from the shelter of stone to stone, making slower progress now. Every so often a CAV would speed past, its droid pilot aiming a surveillance probe into the air. They were able to evade it each time . . .

. . . until they stumbled on a small squad of heavily armed droids. This time, there was no hiding. They heard the metallic click as the droids snapped into attack position.

Blaster fire erupted from the droid squad. Raina reached for the two blasters strapped across her chest and kept up a steady barrage as Ferus charged. Obi-Wan took out his lightsaber and went after the left flank, while Ferus charged toward the right.

Obi-Wan sliced off the head of a droid and used his backswing to disable the control sensor suite of another. Ferus flew through the air and executed a diving roundhouse kick, somehow slipping through the streaks of blaster fire without catching any of it.

The other two droids retreated behind a tall standing stone and began peppering them with blaster bolts.

"Here come the reinforcements." Raina pointed into the distance with her chin, where CAVs were approaching. "If you can dispatch those two, I can get to an open area and activate a smoke grenade. The wind is southeast — it will carry most of the smoke toward the CAVs. I can get us through the smoke to the secret entrance in the wall. That way they won't lock on our position."

"Done." Obi-Wan summoned the Force and leaped to the top of one of the smaller standing stones. He jumped from one to another until he had the droids in view. Then he dropped behind them. Before they had a chance to turn and fire, two strokes of the lightsaber turned them into scrap.

Raina raced to the open area and aimed the smoke grenade. She was still out of range of the cannons on the CAVs. The grenade flew through the air. Thick, acrid smoke billowed out and spread back toward the CAVs. Obi-Wan quickly ran back to the group.

The wind carried much of the smoke away from

them, but they still had to make their way through
it, their eyes streaming. They followed the metallic
sheen of Raina's armor as she led them through the
smoke. When they arrived at what looked like a sheer
wall, she pressed several stones in what appeared to
be a random pattern. One large stone slid out.

She motioned them inside.

"Welcome to Eluthan," she said.

CHAPTER SIX

They walked through the narrow deserted streets. The city wasn't laid out in a grid, but in a random pattern, streets and alleys turning and ascending and descending the hilly terrain. The houses were made of mellow bronze stone, and were only a few stories tall.

"Most of the citizens have evacuated," Raina explained. "This is pretty much just an army base now. But once it was a thriving city."

They walked to a sprawling stone building on the edge of a grassy plaza. The plaza now served as a landing platform for the ships. A plastoid roof sheltered it and connected it to the building.

"This used to be a school," Raina said. "Many of the students joined the resistance, and the rest offered the building as a base for operations. Most Acherins are totally devoted to this cause. We didn't have to ask for sacrifices. They offered them."

Trever smirked. "Or maybe they just wanted to get out of classes."

Raina didn't take offense; she laughed. "Maybe."

Obi-Wan looked around at the low, stately building, the expanse of grass that had once thrived and now was brown and seared with the scorch of afterburn and the trampling of boots. Once, boys and girls had run through this grass, had studied at this school.

Odd how much he hated war, yet how much of his life had been spent around it.

Raina nodded at a guard standing outside the double doors, and she and her guests were allowed in. She quickly led the way to the command center, a circular hall in the middle of the building. It had once been a gathering place for students, Obi-Wan guessed. Now it had been outfitted with vidscreens and computer banks.

A tall man with a shaved head saw them enter. His face was impassive, but Obi-Wan noted how his body relaxed and his gray gaze cleared when he saw Raina. Obi-Wan guessed this was Toma.

"We thought you were shot down," the tall man said.

"They tried," Raina said. "I lost my ship. But I met some friends." She introduced them.

Toma looked at Obi-Wan searchingly. "I am glad to meet a Jedi."

"You knew Garen Muln."

"Yes, we —"

Suddenly the command screen lit up with pulsating lights. Toma turned and regarded the screen. "The counterattack has begun. The Empire has our fleet surrounded. We need to scramble all pilots back up there."

"I'm ready," Raina said. "All I need is another ship."

To Obi-Wan's surprise, Ferus spoke up.

"I'd like to offer my services," he said. "Any chance to take a whack at the Empire, I'm for it."

"We could use your help," Toma said. "Raina, can you find our friend a ship?"

"Ferus . . ." Obi-Wan said, but he didn't know how to finish the thought. He couldn't forbid Ferus to go. That wasn't his place. Ferus wasn't his Padawan.

He would remain here. This was not his fight. He could never forget that his duty was to Luke and Leia. He could take no unnecessary risks.

"Don't fret, Obi-Wan. I'll just do a little damage and come back to get you," Ferus said easily.

"I want to go," Trever said.

"Sorry, kid," Ferus said. "Not this time."

"I'm really getting tired of being left behind."

"I don't think stowaways have a choice," Ferus said.

Toma turned to Obi-Wan. "Will you watch the battle with me? Your advice will be appreciated. I have great respect for the Jedi."

Obi-Wan bowed his head. He would be happy to offer advice, but his heart was heavy. He knew this effort was doomed. Ferus saw his feeling in the Jedi's eyes, and turned abruptly to go with Raina.

Toma began barking out orders to his pilots. Obi-Wan took a moment to familiarize himself with the pattern on the large, square screen on the wall.

"Your left flank is weak," he told Toma. "In battles like this, many commanders like to use pincer movements. They have the superior numbers. You have to fly through them, not around them. It's more dangerous, but it's also more effective."

Toma nodded. He spoke into the comlink, translating Obi-Wan's words into specific ship movements. The dots on the screen reassembled.

Toma pointed to two moving dots, each with a different number code. "That is Raina and Ferus. They've taken off."

Obi-Wan kept his eyes on them. Ferus had made his decision, but Obi-Wan wished he had stayed here. He suddenly realized how much he was depending on him. He himself had to return to Tatooine, but his consolation was that Ferus would be out in the galaxy, doing what he could, where he could.

He had no more advice to give to Toma. It was

clear to him, looking at the screen, that the battle was already lost. The Acherins simply did not have enough ships or firepower. He was amazed at the daring pilots and their skill, but one by one the blinking dots disappeared. Toma's face grew ashen.

"We are losing our best," he said.

"They can't hold out," Obi-Wan said gently.

"We didn't dare to hope that we'd beat them," Toma said. "We hoped we would be enough of a nuisance that they'd just go away."

"They never just go away," Obi-Wan said. "Their reach is a stranglehold. They won't let go."

"If I pull the pilots back, it's over," Toma said. "I will have to surrender Eluthan."

"If it must be done, it should be done," Obi-Wan said.

Toma spoke into his comm unit. "Recalling all pilots," he said. "The battle is lost. Return to base. You have done well, each one of you."

He bowed his head. Obi-Wan watched as Toma struggled with his decision. When he raised his head, his eyes were clear. With Obi-Wan out of view, he contacted the Imperial commander, Admiral Riwwel. Soon Riwwel's face appeared on the screen.

"I am prepared to surrender," Toma said. "I ask for safe passage for my pilots. Acherin agrees to become part of the Empire."

"Do you think after what has happened, after the

many deaths of our forces, that this is acceptable?" Admiral Riwwel sneered. "You must pay for your disloyalty. I do not accept your surrender terms. You will surrender on our terms."

"And what are your terms?"

"Annihilation. Eluthan must pay with its own destruction. Prepare for saturation bombing of the city. We have already knocked out your planetary shield."

Toma whirled to check the computer. "No! It is our ancient city, revered by all Acherins, the site of our most precious treasures!"

"You should have thought of that before you made it your base."

The screen went black.

"What have I done?" Toma wondered aloud.

"You haven't done it," Obi-Wan said. "They have. You must tell the pilots not to return. They'll be destroyed."

"They are almost here . . . they think they have safe passage . . ." It was true. The pulses of light were returning. Behind them were the lights of the Imperial destroyers, tailing them. Toma spoke into the comlink. "Do not return to Eluthan! Repeat, do not return! Take evasive action, now!"

Obi-Wan saw the great Empire's ships fire even as the pilots peeled off. All of them made it, a tribute to the skills of the Acherin pilots. To his dismay, he saw two pulsating lights begin to take evasive action, but not deflect from their course.

"Ferus and Raina are returning here," he said.

"No," Toma said in disbelief. "They'll be slaughtered."

"Trever, come on — we must get to the spaceport," Obi-Wan said.

The sounds of explosions came to them now. The Empire was leading a barrage against the city. Toma flipped the image control and they saw scenes of devastation outside as cannons boomed from the destroyers above.

Toma flinched as a large, stately building suddenly disintegrated. "Libraries, museums . . . our university. How could an invading force do this? They're targeting them. Why can't they just allow us to surrender? This is our civilization!"

"It is yours, not theirs," Obi-Wan said. "So they don't care about it. All they care about is a display of power. Toma, we must go."

Toma snapped back into his authority. "There is a hidden landing platform with my personal transport. That is where Raina will be going."

With a last glance at the screen, Obi-Wan turned. He motioned to Trever. "Stay close to me."

"I'm not going to argue with that," Trever said.

The building shook with the heavy barrage. The

thick stones held up, but cracks appeared and dirt rained down on them as they ran down the corridors.

They heard the sound of thudding boots.

"The stormtroopers are here," Obi-Wan said.

Toma turned down another corridor. The echo of the stormtrooper boots seemed to be everywhere. Obi-Wan focused on the sounds, tuning into the Force to tell him what he needed to know.

"There's a squad of twenty ahead. But only five behind," he told the others, reversing direction. "This way."

"No, we can't," Toma said. "That leads to a dead end. We have to go this way."

Toward twenty stormtroopers? "Oh, well," Obi-Wan said. "You can't have everything."

He charged forward, lightsaber in hand. Toma was at his side with his blaster ready.

Trever called out in a whisper. "Wait!"

Obi-Wan paused impatiently. Trever had opened up a closet marked ATHLETIC EQUIPMENT. He took out a box of laserballs.

"Let me go first. I'll give you the edge you need."

Obi-Wan hesitated. "Trever, I'm not sure about this."

"Trust me."

There was no time to argue. The stormtroopers were approaching.

Obi-Wan stood near Trever, poised to protect him. As the footsteps grew closer, he nodded at Trever.

The stormtroopers appeared, rounding the corner, moving quickly in lockstep. With a flick of his wrist, Trever sent six laserballs shooting down the corridor, centimeters above the floor.

Flick. Flick. Flick. Trever's action was so fast it was almost a blur. More laserballs zoomed down the hallway.

At first, the stormtroopers were just confused. Then they tried to evade the laserballs, but one got tangled up and started to fall. Another crashed into one on his left. Before long, they were colliding, trying to keep their balance and shooting at Obi-Wan and the others at the same time. Blaster bolts pinged through the air and hit the walls and ceiling.

Obi-Wan leaped directly into their midst. While Toma came at them on the right with his blaster, Obi-Wan's lightsaber danced. Within seconds the entire squad had been demolished.

"Thanks for the edge," Toma told Trever.

They continued on. Toma led them through a narrow passage to a small hangar with one ship. He flicked on a vidscreen. The sky outside was thick with Imperial starfighters. "We're underground now. I can activate the opening when we see Ferus and

Raina," he said. "It's concealed in the side of the building."

Obi-Wan looked at the ship. It was a battered star cruiser with dull gray plating.

"I know," Toma said. "It doesn't look like much. It's not supposed to. But it's got a tweaked hyperdrive engine and all the firepower you could want."

"Look!" Trever called, pointing to the vidscreen.

Two ships were spinning and diving, cartwheeling through the air as cannonfire streaked around them. Smoke was spiraling out from one of the ships. Obi-Wan didn't know whether it was Ferus's or Raina's.

Toma pressed a switch as they dove in a straight line toward the surface. At the very moment it seemed they would crash into the city, they veered off. Part of the ceiling overhead slid back, and they dropped into the hangar.

Raina quickly popped her cockpit canopy and leaped out as her ship exploded into flames. Toma and Trever took a step back from the heat, but Obi-Wan raced toward Ferus's ship. Why hadn't Ferus opened the cockpit canopy?

He looked down into the transparent bubble. Ferus was working at the canopy manually with a vibrocutter. When he saw Obi-Wan, he stepped back. Obi-Wan used his lightsaber, and the cockpit canopy peeled back. Ferus leaped out.

"I lost all systems in that last dive," he said. "Even the manual control blinked out. Thanks for the help."

Stormtroopers poured into the hangar, firing as they came. Obi-Wan deflected the fire with his lightsaber as they ran toward the remaining ship. Raina leaped aboard and started the engines. Toma helped Trever up the ramp.

Ferus and Obi-Wan turned their attention to the stormtroopers. Obi-Wan deflected fire and used the Force to push several stormtroopers backward, knocking them into the formation and sending several of them tumbling, hampered by their armor.

Obi-Wan and Ferus took advantage of this to jump aboard. The ship lifted off and streaked outside. Dodging cannonfire, Raina guided the ship through the smoking city.

"I can't believe it," Raina cried. "I can't believe they're destroying the city!"

But she didn't have time for reflection. Starfighters were chasing them, hammering at them with cannonfire.

"They've locked a missile on our position," Obi-Wan called.

"I've got to take us through the standing stones," Raina said.

"Isn't this ship a little big?" Ferus asked. "There's no room to maneuver."

"I've done it before on a training exercise," Raina assured him.

"That was in a starfighter," Toma pointed out. "And you crashed your ship."

"Is he kidding?" Trever asked.

Raina shook her head. "Toma never kids."

"Oh, good." Trever gulped.

Raina flew over the walls that circled the city. She dove down into the canyon of standing stones. She did it so fast that the torpedo crashed into a standing stone with a roar.

Obi-Wan gripped the console as a giant stone came at them. Raina flipped the ship sideways, then zoomed around another stone.

It's almost like flying with Anakin, Obi-Wan thought. For a second, this made him happy. Then he remembered the rest of it, and it pierced him. *Anakin.*

The starfighters overhead dipped down to follow them. One of them tipped a wing into a stone and spiraled out in a fiery crash. The spaces between the stones were so narrow that their starship barely made it through, even when Raina tipped them sideways.

Most of the starfighters gave up and lurked above in airspace, waiting for them to emerge. But one determined pilot swooped behind them. It was a race now, and Raina's face was set with determination. She headed straight for a narrow opening between two standing stones.

"You'll never make that one," Obi-Wan said. Inwardly he thought, *I really do hate flying.*

Raina didn't answer. It seemed as if she meant to kill them all. She still headed for the opening at top speed, the starship behind her screaming through the stone field.

At the last moment, she dove to the ground and cut her speed. Obi-Wan didn't think any ship could handle such a maneuver without stalling out, but this one did. With a great shudder, it hovered only meters off the ground. The starship tried to flip sideways and make the opening between the two stones, but the pilot must have been distracted by Raina's sudden maneuver. It crashed headlong into the stone.

Raina gently eased the ship close to ground level through the rest of the stone field. They were reaching the end of the canyon, and the standing stones were farther apart now.

"The starfighters are still up there," Ferus said, his eyes on the nav screen.

Obi-Wan watched Raina. She was going so slowly. Why?

The sun was slipping down in the sky. Suddenly it hit the stones and lit them with orange fire.

"We call this the flames of Eluthan," Toma said.

At the same time that the stones lit up, the canyon walls surrounding them went deep black with shadow. Raina put on a burst of speed and entered the canyon, losing herself in the shadows.

"This ship has a cloaking device," Toma explained to the others. "It drains a lot of power, so we can't use it for long. In the meantime, we'll make it hard for them to get a visual sighting."

Raina did some amazing flying, pushing the speed and hugging the contours of the canyon wall.

Trever was impressed. "If you ever want to give piloting lessons, sign me up," he said.

Raina only nodded for an answer. Her face was set in grim lines. She knew how slim their chances were to outrun and outfox a squad of Imperial starfighters.

Wide navy blue sky loomed ahead. They were almost out of the canyon. Raina shot out into the dusky sky and headed up into the outer atmosphere, now pushing the speed to maximum.

"We made it!" Trever crowed.

"We're losing the cloaking device," Raina said.

"Just a few . . . more . . . seconds," Toma said, scanning the sky.

But Obi-Wan's eyes were on the screen. He saw the blinking dots reverse direction.

"They've spotted us," he said.

CHAPTER SEVEN

The starfighters were gaining on them. The first missile streaked from the lead starfighter.

Raina pushed the craft left, then right, leading them on a zigzagging path that made them dizzy. The missile zoomed past them on the right.

"Any volunteers for the gun pods?" Toma asked. He flipped a switch, and gun stations opened up below the cockpit.

Ferus and Obi-Wan ran to the forward gun pods and strapped themselves behind the guns. They waited until the starfighters came into range. Ferus felt the Force gather and grow as they pounded the starfighters behind them.

But the starfighters were relentless, and more were sent from the surface. It was clear that the Imperial commanders knew that Toma had escaped on this ship. The starfighters zoomed toward it, grouping and regrouping, and pounding the ship with fire. They took one hit, then another.

"We've got to lose them!" Ferus shouted.

Bent over the nav computer, Toma shook his head. "We're in deep space now. There are no neighboring systems."

"Hold them off for a minute," Obi-Wan told Ferus before running back to the cockpit. Ferus watched him out of the corner of his eye. What was he up to?

"I have an idea," Obi-Wan told Toma. He quickly bent over the nav computer, making a wide search of the area. "On the way to Acherin we were caught in a fast-moving star tunnel. The kind that spins out from a vast atmospheric storm."

"And you want to find the storm?"

Obi-Wan looked up at him. "It's one place to lose the starfighters. We're heavier and more durable. How much do you trust your ship?"

"I trust my ship," Toma said. He glanced at Raina. "I trust my pilot more."

"Here." Obi-Wan found what he was looking for. "If we can hold them off just a little longer, we can make it."

"I'll go to maximum speed," Raina said.

Obi-Wan went back to the gun pods. They kept up a steady barrage of fire. Raina flew fast in a series of dizzying turns and circles.

The ship started to shake alarmingly.

"Coming up on that storm," Toma called. He whistled. "It's a bad one. I've got indications of space shears and shifts."

Space shears could tear apart a class-A cruiser, if a pilot wasn't careful. At the sign of shears, pilots were happy to make detours of thousands of kilometers if they had to.

"We can still get around it," Toma said.

Raina gritted her teeth. "No. This is the only way to shake them. Obi-Wan is right."

They flew straight into the atmospheric storm. The jouncing of the ship turned into a violent bucking.

"She can take it," Toma said to a visibly nervous Trever. "The ship is double-hulled and triple-bolted. We have backups on every system. I built this myself during the Clone Wars. It's not an ordinary starship."

"This isn't your ordinary storm," Trever said as a space shear hit them broadside.

Trever skidded across the cockpit floor and came to rest against the console. He grabbed it and held on.

A current of energy sent them spinning off out of control. Raina went with the spin, letting the ship find its own balance. "The trick with these energy shifts is to fight them as little as possible," she said.

Ferus had to admire her nerve. The hardest thing

for a pilot to do was let the ship take over. Raina watched the indicators, her gaze steady, not interfering with the ship's attempt to right itself. It did no good to fire the cannons. They were spinning too crazily.

"The starships are retreating," Ferus called. "They're more afraid of the storm than they are of their admiral." *Or else,* he thought privately, *they figure that we're doomed.*

Raina began to take over the controls again, easing the ship through the buffeting storm. On and on they flew, slammed by currents of energy that sucked them into vortexes and spun them out like droplets of water. The ship staggered and lurched, sometimes close to stalling out the engines. Ferus started to worry when he noticed that Raina looked concerned.

"We're almost out of it," Toma called in relief.

The ride smoothed out, but suddenly they could see nothing. It was as though a curtain had dropped over the cockpit windscreen. They had entered an atmospheric cloud so dense that space outside was just a gray, roiling mass.

"Even the sensors can't penetrate this," Raina said. "I can't get any readings. There must be some sort of energy field —"

Suddenly Ferus felt something surge, a warning.

"Ferus . . ." Obi-Wan said.

"I felt it." He strained his eyes ahead.

Suddenly an asteroid loomed ahead, seemingly close enough to touch. It had appeared without warning and they were headed straight for it.

"Look out!" Trever shouted.

Raina pulled back on the speed. Just in time, the craft pulled up, and they zoomed just meters above the pitted surface while she desperately searched for a place to land.

"There." Obi-Wan pointed.

Raina skimmed over the rocky ground and gently set the ship down on a large, flat rock.

Raina peered through the cockpit canopy. "Where *are* we?"

Toma scanned the nav computer. "This asteroid should have made it onto star maps. It's large enough, and it has an atmosphere. But there's no trace of it."

Obi-Wan activated the canopy and hauled himself up and out. He looked above. The sky was a dense blue haze. He couldn't see a star.

"I think this asteroid is locked into the force field of the storm," he said. "It can't break out, so it travels constantly as the storm travels."

"And cruisers avoid the storm, so the asteroid isn't mapped," Ferus said, hauling himself up and out of the cockpit to stand beside Obi-Wan. "Let's take a look around."

They explored the area around the ship, but all they found were craters and dust.

"At least we're safe," Raina said. She stretched. "And I could use a rest."

"Yeah, getting pounded by the Empire's starfighters and then pulverized by a galactic storm will do that to you," Trever said. "Not to mention, we missed lunch."

Raina laughed and slung an arm around Trever. "You're starting to grow on me, kid."

"Yeah, just like goblin moss," Trever said.

Raina and Trever headed off to prepare a shelter. Toma turned to Obi-Wan.

"You have been waiting to speak to me," he said.

"Yes," Obi-Wan said. "Tell me about the death of Garen Muln."

Toma looked startled.

"Death?" he said. "But Garen Muln isn't dead . . . he's alive."

CHAPTER EIGHT

"We were together when it happened," Toma said. "At our headquarters in Eluthan. We were negotiating the terms of the truce. That didn't take long, but we were enjoying each other's company. We had thought we were enemies, but we found we had much in common. Then it happened."

"The clone troopers," Obi-Wan said.

"He was in the operations base with me," Toma said. "We had the vidscreens on, and we saw the clone troopers attack. Like someone had thrown a switch — it was clear they had orders to hunt down Garen and kill anyone who got in their way. He wanted to go out and fight, but it was too late. I had to convince him to stay with me, that I could hide him. And I did. I had a secure place in the volcanic caves outside the city, a place I had created in case the worst happened. I never thought the worst would happen to the man who had once been my enemy, and that I would protect him."

"Did they search for him?"

"For weeks," Toma said. "I was interviewed by a special group called the Inquisitors."

"We've heard of them," Ferus said drily.

"Was one of them named Malorum?" Obi-Wan asked.

Toma shook his head. "No. Why?"

I guess all roads don't lead to Malorum, Obi-Wan thought. But that didn't make him any less of a threat.

"It's not important," the Jedi said. "Please continue."

This time, Toma nodded. "Finally," he said, "the Inquisitors gave up. They assumed, I think, that he had escaped the planet. Once things had quieted down a little, Garen told me it was time to go. I gave him a ship."

Obi-Wan could not believe what he was hearing. He had grown used to casualty after casualty after casualty. He had walled himself against hope, as a way of keeping away the inevitable disappointment and sadness. Even though he knew there was a slight possibility that Jedi other than himself and Yoda had survived, with every day the possibility had seemed slighter and slighter, until it seemed a mere thread against the whole weight of the Empire.

But now . . . he felt the hope rise inside his chest, a feeling that was so unfamiliar it felt brand-new. His good friend, Garen. Possibly alive. He was afraid to believe it, but he was desperate for it to be true.

"Do you know where he went?" he asked Toma.

"He was going to make his way to a place called Ilum," Toma said. "He told me that I should only inform another Jedi of this, and they would know why."

Ferus and Obi-Wan exchanged a glance. Ilum was the site of the Crystal Cave, where every Jedi apprentice went to forge his or her own lightsaber. It was sacred to the Jedi.

"Ilum," Ferus said. "Of course." He grew excited. "I never thought of it before. Others could have gone there, too."

"He's probably hiding in the cave," Obi-Wan said, knowing that is what Garen would do: Find a safe place that the Jedi knew better than anyone else.

Toma went to join Raina and Trever and build a shelter. Ferus paced up and down, excited at the news.

"We have to go there," he said to Obi-Wan. "Who knows how many Jedi could be there? There could be more of us than we know."

Ferus didn't even know what he was saying until the word was in the air. *Us*. This was the truth: Even though he had left the Jedi, he still felt like he was one with them. Not one *of* them, but one *with* them.

He could no more disconnect from the Force than he could disconnect from his own thoughts. It was a part of him. He could not deny it. This new hope made the bond even clearer, as if the course of action had shone a spotlight on his attachment.

Obi-Wan did not comment on Ferus's choice of words, but Ferus could see him taking everything in, just as he always had.

"You are not here to be punished, least of all by yourself," Obi-Wan had told him when he approached the Jedi Council for the last time, to resign from the Order.

"I must go on living," Ferus had responded. *"That is my punishment."*

He knew Obi-Wan hadn't wanted him to leave. If he'd been Obi-Wan's Padawan, it would have all been different. Everything would have been different.

But instead Obi-Wan was left with Anakin, and Ferus was left with nothing. Before he'd exiled himself from the Temple, he'd told Anakin, *"If the Jedi ever need me, I will be there."*

Now here he was, among the last of the Jedi.

"You remember the caves?" Obi-Wan asked.

"Of course," Ferus answered. How many times had he and the other Padawans — his friends — talked about the things that happened there, about the tests that would lead to the creation of their lightsabers? His Master, Siri, had taken him there when he was thirteen. She had left him in the caves to fight off his greatest fears — and although it had been terrifying, he had somehow maintained his calm. He made it through, and forged his own blade.

Then, in what seemed like no time at all, he gave up the lightsaber. Let it go.

But not entirely.

"I can forge a new lightsaber," he said now, thinking how helpful this would be. "If I can get the crystals, I can do it again."

Obi-Wan nodded, but he felt hesitant. Ferus was no longer a Jedi. His hold on the Force was growing, but it was still erratic. By the time an apprentice came to the caves at Ilum to find crystals, they were at the peak of their preparation. If Ferus were his Padawan, he would make him wait.

"I know what you're thinking, Obi-Wan," Ferus said. "But you are not a Master, and I am not an apprentice." Ferus's face was flushed. "You seem locked in an old pattern."

"I don't think so," Obi-Wan answered gently. "The caves are a difficult trial, even for a fully prepared apprentice."

"I know that. I've been through them. I know there are things I've forgotten, but I can't wait until I've relearned everything again. Do you really think we can afford to wait? Perhaps Jedi caution is what paved the way for their destruction."

The accusation stung, but hadn't Obi-Wan thought the very same thing?

His own caution . . . it had paved the way for Anakin Skywalker to turn into Darth Vader. He had felt uneasy about his Padawan, but he had never imagined how corrupted he could become. As a Padawan, Ferus had seen something dangerous in Anakin. But Obi-Wan had not done anything about it.

Now he must learn from his mistakes. It was time to be bold.

Obi-Wan was torn. He wanted nothing more than to find his friend Garen alive. But he also knew he had to keep his attention on the real threat — Malorum. On Bellassa they had learned that Malorum had sent an investigator to Polis Massa. Obi-Wan was sure that Luke and Leia's birth had been covered up completely . . . but could he be absolutely certain?

Malorum reported to Darth Vader. Was Darth Vader suspicious about Padmé's death? Was there any path that could lead him to find that she had given birth to Luke and Leia before she'd died?

Obi-Wan had to find the answers to those questions. And he wasn't going to find them in exile on Tatooine.

Or, he realized, in the Caves of Illum.

You must follow your feelings, Qui-Gon had said.

And suddenly, Obi-Wan had a feeling that

Qui-Gon was with him. Free of the constraints of place, trained in the way of the Whills, Qui-Gon could be right beside him, and Obi-Wan wouldn't know except for the feeling that filled him.

If Luke is to rise, he must have something to join, Qui-Gon's voice said in his mind.

Obi-Wan turned to look in the distance, so Ferus wouldn't see his distraction.

Yes, he answered. *You've told me that already. It is why I left to help Ferus.*

If Luke is to rise, he must be protected from those who seek to do him harm.

So I should go to Polis Massa?

You should follow your feelings.

Obi-Wan knew what that meant. *They lead me there,* he told his Master.

So go.

Obi-Wan felt Qui-Gon move from him as quickly as a breeze. One moment he'd been there, the next, gone. But Obi-Wan's decision had been made. He had to trust Ferus to search for Garen . . . while he himself had to go to Polis Massa. He had to ensure that Luke and Leia's secret was safe. If Luke was found, then Ferus was doomed, Garen was doomed . . . they were all doomed to live or die under the Empire. That was what Qui-Gon was telling him.

Ferus had stopped pacing and was watching him. "You don't agree with me."

"I do agree," Obi-Wan said. "You're right. This is your time to be bold. To take the biggest chances."

Ferus looked relieved. "Besides, you'll be with me in the caves."

Obi-Wan spoke slowly, knowing what he was about to say would be a surprise to Ferus. "No, I won't be. I'm not going with you. There's something else I have to do."

"What could be more important than your friend?" Ferus asked incredulously.

Obi-Wan looked at Ferus, helpless to answer. What could he say? Ferus didn't know that Anakin had become Darth Vader, didn't know that Anakin had fathered two children. These were things Obi-Wan was forbidden to tell him, things that Ferus couldn't know. It would only be a burden to him. It was dangerous for anyone else to know.

"All of our fates," Obi-Wan said. "That is more important."

Ferus was now angry. He could see that. Obi-Wan felt frustration. He couldn't fully confide in Ferus, and that would always be between them. He would have to accept that.

"All right," Ferus said stiffly. "I was hoping to have your help, but I can do it alone."

"I'll take you there," Obi-Wan said. "I can drop you and then return for you. Trever can keep watch, and alert me if something goes wrong. The place I'm going isn't far from Ilum, and I hope my time there won't be long."

Ferus gave a short, angry nod. He did not, however, question Obi-Wan further. Obi-Wan appreciated that.

"I can still help you," Obi-Wan said. "You must be careful. If it seems logical to us that Jedi would go to Ilum, then it is logical to the Empire as well. They will have some kind of presence there. But I know another way to the caves, a secret way."

The anger left Ferus's face. He had accepted it and let it go, just as a Jedi should. Suddenly he was all business, focused on the next stage of the mission. "Good."

"Not so good," Obi-Wan said. "The secret way leads straight through a gorgodon nest."

CHAPTER NINE

They stood in front of Toma's ship. Obi-Wan looked around at the bleak landscape. "Are you sure you and Raina want to stay?" he asked Toma.

"We're on the Empire's wanted list now," Raina said. "I'd say this was the safest place in the galaxy for us. We packed the ship with supplies and food, just in case we had to make a quick escape. So we'll be okay here . . . for now."

They spoke lightly, but Obi-Wan knew how much courage it took for them to stay. There was a chance he and Ferus wouldn't be able to find them again.

There was a homing beacon on the ship that they would leave on the asteroid, but there was no guarantee it would work through the atmospheric disturbances surrounding the asteroid. They would test it after they left the atmosphere, but anything could happen.

"We'll return for you," Ferus said. "I'll find you

no matter what, I promise you that. And we'll bring back supplies, in case you decide you need to stay for a time."

Raina looked at Trever. "Are you sure you want to go?"

"It's hard to leave all this," Trever said, waving a careless hand. "But yeah."

He, Obi-Wan, and Ferus boarded the ship. They shot off into space and almost immediately were buffeted by the severe energy storm. Ferus followed the tips he'd gotten from Raina and guided the ship through the energy shifts and shears. The ship jolted and went into a bad roll, but he held on. He was determined to make it through. Toma's ship was the most stable he'd ever flown.

"Homing beacon is holding," Obi-Wan said. "I can access their coordinates."

"Good, we'll be able to get back."

"Sure," Trever shouted as a sudden shift sent them plummeting through space. "If we ever get *out*!"

They flew through the worst of the storm and at last entered calm deep space.

Ferus entered hyperspace in a rush of stars. It would be less than a day's journey to Ilum.

Ferus's disapproval of Obi-Wan's decision hung between them, and they passed most of the journey in silence.

Why was it, Obi-Wan thought, *that he could be sure of a decision, yet be torn by its effects?*

He was sending Ferus into the caves of Ilum alone, with only Trever to stand watch outside. It would be the test of whether Ferus could truly be a Jedi again. The time for rules was gone. There was no more Jedi Council. There was no one to tell Ferus he wasn't ready.

Obi-Wan remembered his conversation with Qui-Gon back on Tatooine.

Speak of what you know about Ferus, not what you can guess, Qui-Gon had said.

Now Obi-Wan thought, *He was the most gifted apprentice, second only to Anakin. With so many gifts, he is a formidable opponent of the Empire.*

With a lightsaber, with a hold on the Force constantly renewing, constantly strengthening, he would be even stronger.

To get through the cave alone, to find Garen, to find crystals . . . it could break him. Or it could make him.

To give in, to trust in another's strength . . . that was something Obi-Wan had once learned, long ago. Anakin had never learned it. In his arrogance, he had thought that he was the only one who could accomplish the hard things.

But Obi-Wan knew there were times he had to

step back and let another go forward. This was one of those times. Even if Ferus never understood, never accepted him.

Even if Ferus failed.

Obi-Wan was at the controls when they reverted to realspace. Ilum lay ahead.

"We'll have to come around on the back side of the planet," Obi-Wan said. "It's good that there's no orbiting surveillance."

"There doesn't have to be," Ferus said. "It's obvious that they don't consider the Jedi a threat."

"Let's get close enough to get a sensor reading," Obi-Wan said. He dipped closer to the planet, pleased at the feel of the controls in his hands. Toma hadn't exaggerated. This was an exceptional ship.

He skimmed low over a glacial lake dotted with icebergs. "I can land on the edge of the lake. Trever can stay here while you hike up the mountain."

Trever looked around dubiously. "Wow. You pick the best spots, Obi-Wan. I can tell this will be fun."

"It'll be better than a nest of gorgodons," Ferus said.

"Is that my only choice?"

"You can always come with me, Trever," Obi-Wan said. "I can leave you someplace safe and come back for you."

He shook his head, as Obi-Wan knew he would. "No, thanks," he said carelessly. "I'm getting used to waiting for Ferus."

Obi-Wan landed the craft. "It's not far, but it's straight up," he said to Ferus. "Remember, you have to progress past the visions. Don't let them stop you. Keep going. The crystals lie in the middle of the cave. If Garen is there, that's where he'll be."

Ferus nodded.

"May the Force be with you."

"And with you."

Ferus and Trever exited the craft. Obi-Wan took off again. He didn't look back. He knew the sight of Ferus and Trever dwindling in the distance would cause him pain. He felt fear clutch his heart, a sudden panic that he wouldn't see them again.

He pushed the speed of the craft toward Polis Massa. Something ticked inside him. Something that told him that he'd better do what he had to do and get back, fast.

Polis Massa was a small mining settlement in the middle of an asteroid field. They had a small but excellent med center, and it was here that the Jedi had found sanctuary for Padmé, at the end of the terrible time when the clone army had turned against the Jedi.

As Obi-Wan descended over the fissured landscape, his heart tightened. He landed Toma's starship in the docking area and took the horizontal lift tube to the surface, walking through the atmospherically adjusted passageways of the planet's inhabitants until he arrived at the med center. With every step, he remembered the terrible day when he'd brought Padmé here. He didn't know she was dying then. He didn't know how badly Anakin had hurt her. Fear had clutched his heart, but he had believed that Padmé, the strong woman he'd known, would survive.

He waved his hand in front of a sensor and entered a small reception area. The med center was primarily run by droids. A screen blinked, and a droid floated into view.

"Please state the nature of your condition."

The nature of my condition is heartbreak.

"I am here to see Maneeli Tuun. Please inform him that it is an old friend."

"Please wait."

The screen blinked off. Obi-Wan paced the confined space. Memories crowded the room, making it seem even smaller. He remembered his helplessness as he carried Padmé inside. He remembered his grief as he watched the Living Force slip from her.

At the end, the med droids did not understand why they couldn't save her, but he had. He believed that Padmé knew her strength was finite. She only had so much left, and no more. And that strength she would give to her children.

She made sure they were born and were healthy. Then — and only then — did she succumb.

He could not do enough for her now. He would fight to his last breath to protect her children. They would someday know of the great courage of their mother.

Obi-Wan and Yoda had barely absorbed the shock of Padmé's death before it was clear to both of them that the best way to ensure the safety of her children was to obliterate any record of their birth. The med droids underwent memory wipes and computer data was expunged. But there was one Polis Massan who Obi-Wan felt he could trust. Maneeli Tuun had been a staunch supporter of the Republic cause and was of unimpeachable character. He had done favors for Yoda over the years and had been one of the reasons Polis Massa had been chosen for the twins' birth. Surely he would help now.

Obi-Wan had no plan yet. He hoped he would find a way to access the med files and make sure that Padmé's records had been erased, just as they'd arranged. That would be the first step.

Maneeli Tuun looked thin and worried when he stepped through the doorway. When he saw Obi-Wan, a look of startled pleasure came over his face but then was replaced by the same frown. "I think I know why you're here. Come."

Before Obi-Wan could say a word, Tuun led him past the inner door and into the hallway of the complex. "We must be careful," he said in a low tone. "He's in the record office."

"Who?"

"Sancor. Isn't that why you are here?"

"Who is Sancor?"

"An Inquisitor."

"I was afraid of that. I didn't realize he was here."

Tuun led him into his small office. "First, an investigator came. He never gave his name, but he copied all our records and took them back to Malorum. That was about a month ago. Now this one arrived. He's an expert on record security. He's already done an exhaustive search on the memory banks of the med droids, even the ones who weren't here during that time."

"Does Malorum know something — does it seem to you that he suspects the truth?"

Tuun shook his head. "I don't think they know anything, but what they *suspect* is another thing. I know they are determined. Now he's asked me for the supply records."

"Why would he want those?" Obi-Wan asked.

"He's going to check the supply usage as well as

waste during the period of time Senator Amidala was here. To see if usage was consistent with the cases."

Obi-Wan was startled. "Would he be able to tell if births took place?"

Tuun frowned. "He might. There are certain tests we do on newborns. Of course we erased all the records and the memory of the droids, but we didn't erase all supply records. When our stocks are low, we do refill orders. The babies were checked over and cared for here, so supplies were used . . . and if he checks various med supplies against patients, he might come up with something. I was just on my way to summon Osh Scal. He's our Polis Massan supply officer — the Inquisitor wants to question him since he's one of the few Polis Massans able to speak. I have no choice. I can only hope that he can't trace anything."

Obi-Wan thought quickly. "Has he seen Osh Scal yet?"

"No, he's been in the record office."

"Can you access the supply records here?"

"Of course. I have access to all records." Tuun quickly called up supply records on the screen. "You see? There are hundreds of items to go through. But he seems determined. And don't think I can erase them here. He will be able to trace it."

"I don't want you to erase anything. But what if you add something? Would he be able to trace that?"

"No."

"All right." Obi-Wan quickly sat down at the console. "Say you had a patient here at the same time as Padmé. Someone who was suffering a great wound from a battle. Can you enter supplies that you would need if they developed complications? Medicines? Special healing devices?"

"Of course. But I don't understand."

"Maybe if we give him a bigger fish to catch, he'll become distracted."

Tuun's troubled expression cleared. "So if he thinks he's on the trail of someone the Empire is looking for . . ."

"Exactly."

"But who?"

"It doesn't matter. We don't need a name. We just need a profile. There are plenty of enemies of the Empire who have gone underground since the end of the Clone Wars, and one of them could have easily fled here. Malorum will try to figure out who it is. The trail will lead nowhere. We just have to plant the seed."

Tuun turned back to the console. "This is sort of brilliant. I think." He keyed in a number of supplies, scrolling through an enormous list. "There. It's buried enough so that he'll have to work to find it. But should we let Osh Scal in on this? He might notice that the supply list is different. He's meticulous."

"No. Sancor hasn't seen him yet. So I'll go."

Tuun copied the files he'd altered onto a disk and handed it to Obi-Wan.

"Obi-Wan, my friend, you must be careful. The Inquisitor is clever." Tuun ran his hands along his cheeks and blew out a tired breath. "I thought we had thought of everything. I checked and triple-checked. The memory wipes are solid. There is no record of the births. There are no records of yourself or Yoda being here. I didn't imagine they would come digging like this."

"They're doing this because they don't have information, not because they do," Obi-Wan said. "Let's go. Maybe I can do something."

Tuun gave a small smile. "If you can send him back where he came from, that would be great. But if he finds out we altered these files, we could both end up executed."

CHAPTER TEN

"You're really leaving me here?" Trever asked, incredulous.

Ferus checked his equipment. "I have to. Only someone who knows how to use the Force can make it through the cave."

"Who said?"

Ferus sighed. "It will make my job harder if you're there, Trever. The visions will confuse and frighten you."

Trever stuck out his chin. "I'm not scared of things that aren't there."

"They are there. Trust me. I don't know if *I* can make it through. And I'm not throwing you into a nest of gorgodons, either. If all goes well, I won't be long. If it doesn't go well . . . wait here for Obi-Wan. And stay out of sight!"

"Stop giving me orders! I'm not a kid!"

"You *are* a kid," Ferus said. "You've seen a lot

and done more, but you're still a kid, and I'm going to protect you when I have to. End of story. Now wait here. If I'm lucky, I'll come out with Garen Muln and a lightsaber."

"And if you aren't lucky, a gorgodon will chew you up and spit you out, and I'll sweep up the pieces," Trever shot back.

"Charming," Ferus said. "Good luck to you, too."

He turned away. He'd only gone a few steps when Trever called after him.

"You'd better make it back!"

Smiling slightly, Ferus moved on. Obi-Wan had showed him the route to the gorgodon nest and the back of the cave. He had even given him tips on how to fight a gorgodon, in case he provoked one.

"Watch out for their tails," Ferus muttered. "And their teeth. And their saliva. And their arms, when they crush you to death."

Ilum was an ice planet, and the snow was as smooth as glass, with an outer layer of permafrost. The air was so cold that he felt as though he'd freeze his lungs with every breath. Ferus had to take small steps and use his liquid cable to haul himself up and over the cliffs.

It was an exhausting climb, and he tried to pace himself despite his eagerness to reach the top. He knew he would need all his strength to meet the gorgodons. He also knew they slept during the day, so he also might make it through the nest without waking them.

As he climbed, he had to shake off a feeling of disbelief that he was here at all. Meeting Obi-Wan again had catapulted him onto a path he hadn't expected. He had left his adopted homeworld, left his partner Roan, all to go on a quest to save any Jedi he could find. And he wasn't even a Jedi any longer!

He wasn't sure what he was anymore. He was a strange creature, half-Jedi, half-man. A space carnival creature for children to point at and laugh, waiting for him to turn into one or the other.

Focus, Ferus, he told himself sternly.

Ferus shot his liquid cable and it pulled him up the remaining hundred meters to the next crag. Thick undulating curtains of ice coated the mountain. Obi-Wan had explained that it would be difficult to pinpoint the location of the gorgodon nest. He would have to use the Force.

Ferus closed his eyes for a moment. It was sometimes an effort for him to clear his mind, to reach out to the Force. Yet using the Force had to be effortless; he could not *try*. He could only exist in this moment, not hope for what was to come. He felt in the air the vibrations of the ice, the rock, the molecules of the sky, his own body. They all existed together in one seamless hum of energy, and from them rose what linked him to everything in the galaxy: the Force.

He felt it gather, and he opened his eyes. Immediately he saw that what he thought was a thick impenetrable curtain was actually a constructed wall. The gorgodons had moved the sheer planes of ice as if it were transparisteel, mimicking the steep slope of the crag for camouflage.

Once he saw this, the rest was easy. Ferus saw the difference in blue shadow and curve of ice. There was an opening in the wall, impossible to see even if one were looking carefully. He walked toward it.

The Force gave him no warnings, but he knew the creatures were near. He could sense them. He walked through the opening and stopped short, confused by what was around him. It took him a moment to make sense of the shapes. The gorgodons had made the nest using ice and boulders to construct shelters that looked like the humped backs of the creatures themselves. They were fifty or so meters tall and hunched together like ascending hills. They used their sticky brown saliva as a kind of mortar to hold the structures together. It had an elastic quality and hung down over the openings, looking like a ruffle on a dainty curtain and swaying slightly in the breeze.

He knew gorgodons had an excellent sense of smell. None of them stirred as he counted the ones he could see. Two on the side, sleeping out in the open. One smaller gorgodon, half in, half out of its shelter. He did not know how many others lay inside the shelters.

There was nothing to do but walk right into the middle of the nest. He saw the opening to the cave ahead, just a slit in the wall, not big enough for a gorgodon to get through. If he could make it through the opening, he would be safe from them.

He started across the nest. A gorgodon stretched and flopped close, and he had to leap out of the way. Which unfortunately entangled him in the foul-smelling, sticky saliva hangings over its shelter. Silently, Ferus fought to extricate himself. It was like being trapped in the thick sap from a tree.

The gorgodon opened one lazy eye. The eye was yellow, and Ferus saw himself reflected in the enormous dark pupil.

He looked very small. And, he imagined, tasty.

The gorgodon opened its mouth and roared, its triple row of yellow teeth still tinged with pink from its last kill. Ferus's blood was already cold, and now it turned to ice. The other gorgodons stirred, and suddenly the air was filled with their cries.

There was a time to fight, and a time to run. He ran.

The tail came out of nowhere, smacking him in the back like a too-friendly hello. This particular greeting made pain ratchet through his body and sent him airborne, flying toward another gorgodon, jaws open to catch and no doubt break him in half.

If ever he needed the Force, it was now. Ferus reached out, but he met nothing, no current that could help him. He knew he was too focused on the jaws that awaited him. The present moment wasn't too awful — he was merely flying through the air. It was the next moment that was the problem. The one where the rows of teeth razored him into slivers.

Instead of reaching for the Force, he reached out for the stringy, elastic saliva looped over the shelter as he flew by. He grabbed at it with desperate fingertips, and it yielded to him.

All he needed was a break in his momentum, and he got it. He pulled on the thick gummy substance, and it boomeranged him backward. He slammed into the side of a boulder, but at least that was better than landing in a gorgodon's jaws.

The gorgodon let out a howl of anger at the diversion of his lunch. He bounded after Ferus. But Ferus was already moving, keeping an eye out for those lethal tails. The gorgodon's hide was so thick that blaster bolts couldn't kill them, only annoy them, so he kept his blaster holstered. He needed to get to the vulnerable spot behind their necks to kill them, and he'd just as soon not get that close. Besides, he was the intruder. He had entered their nest, and he supposed that they had every right to be annoyed with him.

But did they have to be so *mean* about it?

He used the next gummy trail as a swing to lift him over a gorgodon's back. A paw as big as a gravsled tried to swat him, but suddenly the Force was with him, and he sailed above it. He felt the Force now, and he used it to extend his jump over the final gorgodon shelter.

He was almost to the cave opening when he felt himself lift into the air. His first thought was surprise. *I am in the air again, but I didn't jump*, he thought, dazed.

Then the pain hit. The left side of his body was on fire. He realized that he'd been hit with a gorgodon paw. Not only that, but the blow had been perfectly aimed. He was on a straight trajectory to the other paw, which was lifted in wait. He saw quite clearly that the creature meant to whack him from one paw to another, batter him senseless, pop him in his mouth, and crunch.

Not his idea of a pleasant afternoon. Or a decent demise.

Ferus somersaulted in midair, the pain forgotten as the urge to survive surged. He was conscious of the clarity of the cold air, the crystal beauty of the ice, the smell of the gorgodons, rich and fetid in his nostrils.

His boots thudded into the gorgodon's massive palm. His knees bent, and he vaulted off, using the creature's power to send him flying. But instead of allowing the gorgodon to dictate his direction, Ferus used the Force to catapult himself up to the gorgodon's head. He landed in the fur, so slick with ice it was like the slope of a hill. Ferus slid down the creature's neck, slipping his vibroblade out of his tunic and, with a quick swivel of his body, used all his body strength to bury it in the soft place behind the creature's skull.

The bellow of the wounded animal rang through the air and he shook Ferus off like a dry leaf. Again Ferus flipped into the air, but he landed safely on the ground. He took off for the cave as the creature rolled on the ground, trying to dislodge the vibroblade.

He slipped inside the cave opening and was plunged into darkness. He'd made it. The gorgodons were behind him, but he knew the worst still lay ahead.

CHAPTER ELEVEN

Trever wrapped himself in a thermal blanket and sat with his back against an ice-slicked boulder. His breath frosted in the air, so he puffed out a few clouds and watched the vapor dissipate. He did it again. Then he closed one eye and tried to figure out where the ice stopped and the frozen lake began.

Never a dull moment.

Ferus had left him behind again. Just when there was a promise of some action, he was parked like a training scooter. He hadn't expected this. When he'd stowed aboard the cruiser, he hadn't known what to expect, but it certainly wasn't this. He just wanted to escape his homeworld and the Empire — and instead, he was tangled up with Jedi. Okay, he'd been able to see a bit of the galaxy, but hanging around with a resistance hero and a Jedi sure didn't pay well. To Trever's mind, adventure should mean some sort of score along the way. What else was danger for?

Who knew Ferus would turn out to be so . . . noble?

He still liked Ferus, but he didn't sign on to be the moon to his planet.

Trever munched on a protein pellet. Maybe he should split off from these guys and find a nice planet somewhere, someplace out in the Outer Rim where the Empire's reach wasn't quite so . . . grasping. Some decent place that was crying out for a little black market action, where he could buy and sell in peace. Someplace a harmless thief like himself could make an honest living without an Imperial boot in his face.

Was that ice cracking, or a footstep? Trever stopped crunching on his pellet. It certainly couldn't have been the wind ruffling any nonexistent leaves on this frozen wasteland of a planet. No, it was definitely what he thought it was . . . a footstep.

Rolling himself more securely into the concealing thermal blanket, he slid behind a boulder. Directly below him a narrow path curved around the slope. In another second he saw two stormtroopers in some sort of snow gear walking toward him.

He saw at once that they weren't looking for anything. They were just two soldiers, walking a perimeter, doing a boring job.

But they were nowhere near their base. And that meant they'd left a vehicle somewhere near. Which could be a very interesting situation.

Quietly, Trever slipped out of the thermal blanket. He waited until the stormtroopers had disappeared from sight and then slid down the slope. He trudged through the snow, heading back the way the stormtroopers had come.

It didn't take him long to find their transport. Trever let out a low whistle. *Sweet.* It was a small space cruiser. No doubt it was outfitted nicely. He could use some decent food, maybe a few tools or an easily lifted auxiliary booster . . . just a few things they wouldn't notice were gone.

The ramp was still down. Talk about a gracious invitation. Trever walked up and slipped inside the ship.

First he raided the galley and wolfed some food down while he searched. He slipped a brand-new fusioncutter into his pocket — you never knew when one could come in handy — as well as a small pair of electrobinoculars. He took a couple of handfuls of drills for the fusioncutter, just in case he needed them.

He hesitated over a tracomp sensor, but decided they might miss it. He didn't want to leave any evidence of his presence. But he pocketed a handful of alpha-plus chargers he found in a toolbox. They were powerful explosives, usually used in mining. No doubt the troopers needed them to blast through any rocks that got in their way.

Trever thought there'd at least be a couple of spare credits lying around, or some sort of portable currency. There wasn't even a credit chip to pocket. But his pockets were bulging anyway, and it was time to go.

Suddenly he heard the crackle of a transmitter. The stormtroopers were returning. Trever looked out. They weren't in sight yet.

He was just about to race down the ramp when he noticed out of the corner of his eye that a transport was landing. They'd see him if he exited now. Cursing his bad luck, Trever faded back and hovered by the top of the ramp.

The stormtroopers approached the new craft just as it landed. The dome roof of the cockpit opened and Trever clearly heard the officer inside ask, "Anything unusual?"

"Nothing to report," one of the stormtroopers said.

"Return to base. Attack scenario seven implemented."

"Another drill?"

"Negative. A ship was spotted. Sweep indicated a life-form near the vicinity of the cave. You're sure you didn't spot anything unusual?"

"Yes, we're sure."

Just then, one of the drill bits stuffed into Trever's tunic pocket fell out. It bounced with a metallic *ping*, then rolled down the runway.

He just *knew* it didn't pay to be so greedy.

There was a split-second pause. Then the stormtroopers wheeled, searching the area. The sensors in their helmets flashed red as they got a fix on him.

They charged, their blasters pointed straight at Trever.

Quickly he closed the ramp and jumped into the cockpit. He'd once won a hotwiring competition among the youngest thieves of Bellassa. Now he halved his record time.

It was time to go for a ride.

CHAPTER TWELVE

Sancor was a small humanoid whose dark robe seemed to dwarf him. His fingers were long and triple-jointed, and they moved easily over the keyboard as information flooded the screen.

"This is Osh Scal, our medical supply officer," Tuun said, indicating Obi-Wan, who had changed into the appropriate clothes for a medical supply officer, including a face-covering surgical mask.

"At last." Sancor waved Obi-Wan forward without turning to look at him. "I've been waiting for fifteen minutes."

"I was on my break," Obi-Wan said, keeping his tone friendly. "How can I help you?"

Sancor snapped his long, flexible fingers and then held out his hand. "Your supply records covering the dates I indicated. Remain here while I go through them. I'll have questions."

"I'll try to answer them." Obi-Wan handed Sancor the disk that Tuun had given him.

Sancor slipped it into the readout slot. Information sprang to the screen, numbers and letters and codes.

Obi-Wan leaned forward as Sancor scrolled through the material.

"If you tell me what you're looking for, I might be better able to assist you," Obi-Wan said.

"I haven't asked you a question," Sancor snapped. His small black eyes flitted over the material. "Dr. Naturian, I don't remember asking you to stay. I'm sure you have duties elsewhere. A patient to save, perhaps."

"Yes. I'll go, then." With a final look at Obi-Wan, Tuun backed out of the room.

"Here." Sancor's long finger rested a fraction of space away from the screen. "A vitals scan kit. You ordered several replacement kits here."

"Yes, it's an item we use frequently . . ."

"But these are used specifically for newborns to scan for potential problems."

"No, not exclusively."

"There were no newborns in this facility at that time."

"I don't know, I haven't cross-referenced with patient records —"

"But I have." Sancor kept scrolling through.

Suddenly, he stopped. "What is . . ." he closed his mouth. Obi-Wan watched his face. He had discovered the items that Tuun had entered. Sancor licked his lips as he studied the screen. Obi-Wan could see that he was trying not to show his excitement. "You had only a few patients in the med center during this period. Only one was seriously injured. Yet these supplies show a major catastrophic illness was treated. Your records don't reflect that."

Obi-Wan shrugged. "Records can get sloppy."

Sancor gave him an icy look. "Odd that you disparage your own abilities. These records are meticulous. And the med droids are programmed to enter all of their procedures. They should match."

"I'm not a doctor," Obi-Wan said. "I'm just a technician. Maybe you'll want to check the med droids."

"If I wanted to talk to a med droid, I would summon it. Who else had access to your ordering at that time?"

"I do the ordering."

"Does anyone check your orders or see them after you submit them?"

"No."

Sancor looked at him, not believing him. The long fingers stroked the keys. "Let's check the employee list."

One by one, names and photos popped up. Suddenly Obi-Wan felt uneasy.

"I'm sure I can help you," he said. "I just need to familiarize myself with some details."

"Surely you can remember something that happened so close to the end of the Clone Wars."

"It was a chaotic time."

"On the contrary. Things were slow in this quadrant; you were an adjunct on an archeological dig. The action was elsewhere." Sancor turned and looked at Obi-Wan, his antennae twitching.

Behind Sancor's head, the name OSH SCAL popped up, together with a likeness not at all like Obi-Wan's. All Sancor had to do was turn and he would see the truth, that Obi-Wan was impersonating the supply officer.

Obi-Wan reached out for the Force.

"You've seen enough for now, and I can go," he said.

Sancor shook his head. "I have certainly not seen enough."

Sancor's mind was too strong to influence. But Obi-Wan had to prevent him from turning.

Obi-Wan stood up abruptly. "I can access the files more quickly on the other port."

"Then do it."

He almost got away with it. But Tuun suddenly poked his head in. "Are you almost done?"

Sancor swiveled to see Tuun, and his gaze swept the screen. He saw the name and the image.

When he turned back to Obi-Wan, he had a blaster in his hand.

"Suppose you two tell me what's going on," he said. He smiled, and they saw small, pointed teeth. "I didn't know if you had something to hide. But now I'm sure."

Obi-Wan felt the surge of the dark side of the Force before it happened. He activated his lightsaber just as Sancor fired at Tuun. Obi-Wan was able to deflect the fire as Tuun leaped back. Some of the blaster bolts streaked through the air and thudded into the wall. Obi-Wan sprang forward, his blaster activated and ready. He saw the flare of surprise in Sancor's face, and then he ran, brushing past Tuun and taking off down the hallway.

"He's heading toward the main hangar," Tuun said. "We can't let him go. He has the disk!"

Obi-Wan took off. Sancor threw back the sleeves on his robe, and Obi-Wan saw the glint of a wrist rocket.

"Get down!" he yelled to Tuun, even as he dived for cover.

The rocket exploded, sending chunks of the ceiling raining down on his head. Obi-Wan rolled out of the way and charged.

Sancor followed the rocket blast with a barrage of blaster fire. Obi-Wan swung his lightsaber, deflecting the fire.

Sancor raced through a doorway, and Obi-Wan followed. He found himself in a dark, oval room. It took a moment for him to get his bearings, and then he realized that he was on an observation platform high above one of the new operating theaters below. The platform was thrust out from the main corridor and held seats for observers as well as vidscreens and computer consoles.

The empty seats were ghostly in the dim light. He could not see Sancor, but he felt his presence. He did not bother to strain his eyes. Instead he called on the Force and listened.

There, in one corner of the room. Sancor was hiding. Waiting.

He heard the hiss of the wrist rocket before it fired. He jumped aside as it whistled past. It blew a hole in the wall as big as a door. But Sancor had underestimated the power of the missile and the structure of the observation platform. The platform began to tip on its supports.

Obi-Wan made a diving leap toward the hole blown in the wall. He somersaulted through it and landed on the corridor floor as the platform tore away from the wall.

Sancor screamed and scrabbled at a console, desperately trying to make his way to the corridor as the floor tilted under his feet.

The platform slowly broke away from the wall. Sancor lost his grip and fell through the air.

Obi-Wan made his way to the edge of the hallway that ended in midair. He looked over the lip of the floor. Sancor had landed far below on a tray of sharp medical instruments.

It was over. Sancor was no longer a threat.

Slowly, Obi-Wan rose to his feet. Sancor's death wouldn't help matters. Malorum would wonder why he hadn't returned.

Either Padmé's secret was safe, or Obi-Wan had put it in greater peril than ever.

CHAPTER THIRTEEN

The darkness of the cave began to gray at the edges. Ferus's eyes adjusted to the lack of light. The cave walls glowed slightly from the crystals embedded in their rocky surface. Pictographs on the walls told stories of Jedi exploits from thousands of years before. Jedi or no, he was part of that tradition.

The Crystal Cave. They had whispered about it as Padawans and had longed to see it. He remembered his journey here with Siri, when he'd come to build his own lightsaber. He had been tormented by the visions, had at one point curled into a ball to escape them. They had accused him of being on the run from his own true nature, of avoiding the Living Force because he was afraid of himself. They said he only pretended humility, that his prowess as the best apprentice pleased him too much.

They showed him a vision of himself in a torn Jedi tunic, his lightsaber broken, and he had known they were showing him that he would never be a Jedi. At the time he'd thought they were warning him that he wouldn't pass the trials. Now he knew that the vision had come true. He had not become a Jedi Knight.

Back then there was only one who could surpass him — Anakin Skywalker. The visions had told him that jealousy blinded him, and prevented him from being Anakin's friend. He had seen a dark figure in a cape that had frightened him.

I'm waiting for you, Ferus. I lie in your future, the vision had said in an odd, disembodied voice. He had been terrified by that more than anything else.

Now he understood what he'd seen. Possible futures, glimpses into his own fears. He'd only found freedom when he left the Jedi. Freedom to be himself. Roan had taught him that. Roan had taught him not to care what anyone thought, but to regard everyone's feelings. It was a distinction he had somehow not been able to learn at the Temple. He had been too busy trying to be perfect.

He knew now that he hadn't been jealous of Anakin, but he had been afraid of him. Why? He still didn't know the answer to that question.

And what did it matter? Anakin was dead. Like all the others.

He was older now. No longer a Jedi. What visions could come to him now that would frighten him? He had been through a war. He had been scared down to his boots and kept on walking.

He knew himself. He knew his limits and he knew his capabilities. The cave couldn't scare him anymore.

"You think so?"

A shimmering image appeared before him. Ferus's breath caught. Siri. His Master, his friend.

"Here's the thing," Siri said. Even though her image shimmered and fractured, the voice in his head was pure Siri — direct, a little mocking. "You haven't changed a bit. Listen to you — you're still telling yourself that nothing can touch you, that you're the *best*. Is it so important to be the best, Ferus?"

He shook his head. That wasn't what he was thinking.

Was it?

"Is that why you left us? Because you weren't the best, and you knew it?"

"No," Ferus said. "That isn't why I left."

Siri crossed her arms and leaned back, but there was nothing to lean against. She stayed oddly propped against the air, her booted feet crossed. "You don't have to be afraid of what *we* are. You have to be afraid of what *you* are."

"I'm not afraid," Ferus said aloud, even though he knew Siri was just a vision. It seemed pretty stupid to argue with a vision, but there was no other way through. "I know myself now. I didn't then."

Siri's snort of laughter brought him the pain of her absence. But somehow this time her mockery wasn't leavened by affection. It felt harsh to him. "Well, you should be afraid. You're still fooling yourself!" Suddenly she leaned forward. "You want to save the Jedi, all by yourself? Make up for leaving us?"

"No, that's not why!" Ferus said. "I only want to help, I want to fight the Empire!"

"You want to go back and change your decision," Siri said. "You want to be a Jedi again. I've got a Holonet newsflash for you — you can't! You'll never be a Jedi again! All those minor attempts to use the Force — it's pathetic! What did I always tell you? In your plans lie responsibilities. You're forgetting that. Again!"

Siri began to laugh. Her features suddenly fragmented into pieces of light. Then her face reassembled in an odd way, as though her features didn't go together. It was some faceless monster, some image of the dark side of the Force that had appeared to him. How had he forgotten that, the way the images shifted shape until he didn't know who was a Jedi and who was the dark side of the Force?

Or was he projecting what he saw? Were his fears creating the vision?

Fears he hadn't even known were there.

Suddenly, Ferus wished he had decided to do anything else — confront the Emperor himself — instead of entering this cave.

He had done it for Garen, for a Jedi he hadn't even been close to. Someone he couldn't remember very well, a flash of a smile, an ease with the Living Force, an amazing pilot, Obi-Wan's friend.

That was enough. The surge of feeling that came when he thought of Garen taught him something. He must still be a Jedi, there must be a part of him that still vibrated with the Force, if he felt that connection. Garen's life was his life. It was as simple as that. What he had forged in his childhood still rang in his bones.

He walked on, deeper into the cave. Now the walls grew irregular with the chunky crystals that were embedded in the rock. Ferus knew that it would not help him to study the crystals, to find the most beautiful. He must allow the crystals to call to him. If the Force was strong in him, the crystals he needed would speak to him among the thousands that lay around him. *Wait. The right ones will appear.*

He felt awed, being in this spot. Suddenly it came over him, the fact that he was here. Whether he liked it or not, he was on the Jedi path again.

"Unbelievable."

It was Anakin Skywalker. For a moment, Ferus

thought it was really him. He seemed so solid, so real. Then he realized that Anakin was young, probably about sixteen, the age they were when Ferus had left the Jedi.

"It's so like you," Anakin said, "to think that you're the only one who can do something. That ego of yours. No wonder nobody ever liked you."

Ferus waited. He knew this was an image, that he couldn't fight it, couldn't argue with it. And he'd long ago come to terms with what Anakin thought of him. This wasn't anything he hadn't heard before.

"Your jealousy destroyed your future," Anakin said. "You tried to destroy mine, and that didn't work, so you quit."

"You knew Tru's lightsaber was faulty," Ferus said. He couldn't help it. The words had been bottled up for so many years. Ferus and Anakin had both put their friend Tru at risk — and even though Ferus hadn't meant to, he'd accepted the blame. "You were jealous of our friendship, so you said nothing. You hoped we'd get in trouble with the Council. And we did. You knew we wouldn't step forward and tell the truth about you. And we didn't. So you kept your silence, and your place in the Jedi, and you let me walk away from it all."

Anakin shrugged. "Is that your version?"

"It's the truth. And the funny thing is that it was the best thing that happened to me. I found myself."

"Right," Anakin said. "So I hear. Yet I found myself, too."

Suddenly the crystals dimmed. Ferus couldn't see the walls of the cave any longer. A wind moved through the cave.

Wind? Ferus thought. *Where is the wind coming from?* He felt the coldness of fear enter him.

You think you know what fear is?

The whispers began.

Evil was in the cave. He knew it by the icy hand that clutched his heart, by how the strength drained out of his legs.

Had he blundered? Had the dark side of the Force taken over the cave?

Out of the darkness a shadow grew. It was a thing, not a person. A shadow filled with cruel pain. Then the shadow formed and re-formed, and he saw it was a figure. A dark helmet and cape.

Breath entered the cave. A harsh, artificial sound. He heard the indrawn breath, the exhale. It was as though the creature breathed in the darkness and breathed it out.

Darth Vader.

CHAPTER FOURTEEN

He had heard of him, of course. The Emperor's enforcer. The one who came down with an iron fist. And now Ferus knew he was a Sith.

The voice was low and chilling.

"It is our destiny to meet. It is my chore to tell you about the truths from which you hide. You are not a Jedi. You will delude yourself that you are. But then, you have always deluded yourself. You might as well give up now. Because you will fail. And you will bring everyone down with you. Watch."

Ferus saw the vision clearly. Garen, another Jedi who he couldn't place, and, oddly, Raina. And Roan was there, too. They were looking up at a fireball in the sky. As he watched, the fireball consumed them.

He wanted to cry out, but he couldn't.

"In your plans lie responsibilities," Darth Vader said. "But you never think of that, do you? Just your own glory."

In the middle of his fear, Ferus felt a stubbornness rise, and he grabbed it. The Force was here, and he knew that, even if at the moment he was too afraid to access it. Just knowing it still existed in this cave gave him hope.

With the beginning of hope came courage.

He had almost forgotten this. The Force was everywhere, even where evil breathed.

"These are things that can happen," he said. "I can make my own path."

"You have *never* seen the truth."

"If this is your truth, give me my illusions."

Ferus walked forward, straight toward Darth Vader. He was afraid, but he accepted his fear and kept going. If this was to be the end of him, then he would accept it.

The instant he touched the dark cloak, he felt as though he'd been burned. A cry was torn from his throat and he was flung through the air. He hit the ground and moaned.

The dark side of the Force retreated. He felt it sucked out in a vortex.

He was alone.

Through the mist of pain he saw a trio of pale blue crystals, glowing like stars. He struggled to his feet and walked toward them. He put his hand on them, and they were warm. They fell into his hands.

He tucked them into his tunic pocket. He would

have to fashion a handgrip somehow. He wasn't sure how he would do it without the resources at the Temple, the access to design archives, special tools, and power cells. The crystals were the most important, however. He could figure out a way to do the rest.

But the visions weren't done with him yet. Another vision appeared, an ancient Jedi slumped against the cave wall, his tunic tattered, his eyes closed. It was as though he held the defeat of all the Jedi in his shrunken frame.

Ferus walked toward the vision. He would confront this, too. The sound of his footsteps echoed softly. The vision raised its head.

"Who are you?" it asked.

It was real. It was a man.

Ferus slowly lowered himself to a crouch. "Garen?"

Through cracked lips, the man asked, "Who wants to know?"

"I'm Ferus Olin."

"I know . . . that name. Siri's apprentice."

"Yes. We met once . . . long ago. I'm a friend of Obi-Wan Kenobi's."

"Obi-Wan. He's alive?"

"Yes, very much so. He's too stubborn not to be."

Garen leaned back against the rock wall of the cave and smiled. "Yes, now I know it's really you, Ferus."

"He sent me here to find you. He's coming back with a ship."

"Oh, great," Garen said. "Obi-Wan is going to rescue me. I'll never hear the end of it."

"Everybody has a price to pay for survival." Ferus grinned.

"We didn't think any other Jedi had survived."

"We?"

"Fy-Tor-Ana. She came here, too . . . but she was going to make it back to Coruscant, see what had happened to the Temple, and come back for me. She never . . . made it back."

Suddenly, they heard a terrible noise, a howl of agony. And then the air was filled with horrible cries.

"Visions?" Ferus wondered.

Garen struggled to sit. "No."

"The gorgodons," Ferus said. "But why would they be — I'll be right back."

"I'm not going anywhere."

Ferus dashed back through the cave to the opening. He put his eye to the slit.

Stormtroopers with flechette launchers and flame projectors were systematically destroying the gorgodon nest. The creatures fought back ferociously, but Ferus could see that they were only minutes away from defeat. They fought to protect their shelters, but Ferus saw how the stormtroopers were aiming fragmentation grenades at the boulders and outlying walls to create a shower of debris outside the cave entrance. Even as he watched, a large boulder fell directly in front of him, wiping out his view and sending a cloud of pulverized stone into the cave. Coughing, he backed up.

They knew he was here. They were cutting off his exit. He would have to go out the front of the cave now.

He hurried back to Garen. "We have to leave through the front. They'll be waiting there for us, I'm sure." Ferus fumbled at his utility belt. He took out a flask of water and a protein pellet. "Can you swallow this?"

But Garen merely looked at it. He turned his gaze to Ferus, and Ferus saw resignation there.

"You must go. I came here to be with the Force, to rest with the visions of my ancestors. The Living Force is too weak in me now." He struggled to extract his lightsaber from his belt. He handed it to Ferus. "It needs new crystals. I saw you find yours — the blue ones. Put them in. It's yours now."

"I can't take this," Ferus said.

"You must," Garen said. "I will never use it again. It would make me proud to hand it to a fellow Jedi."

"But I'm not even a Jedi. Not anymore."

"I feel the Force in you," Garen said. "That's enough."

Ferus handled the lightsaber reverently. Oddly, the handgrip felt perfectly balanced in his hand. Even though it was nicked and battered, and a large dent was in one side, it nestled in his palm as though he'd fashioned it himself. He touched the latch on the handle and placed the crystals inside. He activated it and the shaft hummed to life, glowing a pale ice-blue.

"Use it well," Garen said.

"I will. I'm going to get us out of here." Ferus leaned down and looked Garen in the eye. "The Living Force may be weak, but it's still in you. It wouldn't be right to leave you without trying. It would be against the Jedi code." He held out the water and the pellet. It took a long moment, but Garen nodded.

Ferus helped Garen sip the water and swallow the pellet. Then he helped him to his feet. Together, they moved toward the front of the cave. Ferus didn't know how he could fight and protect Garen, but he knew it must be done.

He wondered where Trever was. He wondered where Obi-Wan was. He wondered how he had gotten himself into this predicament. He wondered why he couldn't just find a nice planet for a comfortable exile and try to ignore the Empire. He wondered if the visions were right, if he was taking on this task just to prove he was a Jedi after all.

As they approached the opening to the cave,

Ferus moved Garen to the far side, near a large rock. "Stay here while I check this out."

He crept forward. Just as he feared, there was a full squad of stormtroopers lined up outside in battle formation. He counted fifteen. Not an impossible number for one Jedi, but one Jedi who hadn't used a lightsaber in a long time might have a problem.

He watched them for a moment, trying to figure out their plan.

And then he knew what it was.

Behind the troops, a Merr-Sonn Mobile Grenade Mortar was angling into position. It was capable of firing a total of one hundred grenades every second or so, with storage of more hundreds of grenades that could be reloaded through a tube. Operated by two stormtroopers on a repulsorlift sled, it could accelerate fast and rise up in the air to thirty meters. In short, it was highly maneuverable, a deadly killing machine.

Garen had somehow found the strength to creep up beside Ferus. He let out a low whistle. "This is not good news."

"They mean business," Ferus agreed.

"So, how good are you with that lightsaber?"

"Actually, I'm a little rusty."

"I wish I hadn't heard that."

"Do you have any other weapons?"

"No."

"Take my blaster pistol."

"What's your plan?" Garen asked.

"I'm supposed to have a plan?"

"Well," Garen said, "I'd suggest one. Let's refer to our Temple training."

"A quiz? Now?" Maybe he hadn't missed the Jedi so much after all.

"When you meet overwhelming force and you're outnumbered, what are the strategies available to you?"

"Retreat, for one," Ferus said, his eyes on the stormtroopers. "That's always a favorite."

"Impossible in this situation, I'm afraid. Let's try number two."

"Turn the enemy's advantage into yours." Ferus found the words coming easily to him. He remembered sitting in classes at the Temple, studying scenarios. It was thought that even though the Jedi were peacemakers, they should have a knowledge of military strategy. It had served him well as an officer in the Clone Wars. "Capture the grenade mortar," he said slowly. "But how?"

"I came to this cave many years ago to find my crystals," Garen said. "I decided to wait outside until I was ready, until I felt the Force grow around me. Well, that's what I told myself. Actually, I was stalling. I sat for a long time, just studying the cave opening. And I noticed something — a bird. It was one of those tiny white snowfeather birds, and it had built a nest over the cave opening. And I saw that I'd been looking at the cave wrong — it looks as though it's carved out of the face of the mountain, but actually, there's a little overhang above it."

"I'm not getting this," Ferus said. "And I don't like to remind you, but there's a troop of stormtroopers and about a hundred grenades sitting out there."

"The overhang is big enough for a snowfeather nest, but it's also big enough for a man to perch," Garen said.

"Perch?! I don't want to perch! I'd be one big target."

"You can get up there by concealing yourself behind the boulders just inside the entrance," Garen went on. "Climb up the side of the cave, then swing yourself out and into the ledge outside. If you do it quickly, you might not be spotted."

"*Might* not?"

"They won't be looking above the cave, they'll be looking into it, trying to spot movement. Then you can Force-leap over the first columns and land close to the mobile mortar. When they spot you, I'll try to divert their attention."

Ferus looked at Garen dubiously. He looked as fragile as the snowfeather he spoke of. This was the craziest plan he'd ever heard.

But he didn't have a better one.

And time was running out.

"They're going to advance," Garen said, watching. "Let them. You go after that grenade mortar. I'll stay here to meet them."

Ferus looked at him incredulously. "Alone?"

"I won't be alone," Garen said. "The visions will help me. Now go! And may the Force be with you."

Was this the right plan, or was he just used to listening to Jedi Masters? Ferus kept to the side of the cave as he approached the entrance, pressing himself into the shadows until he merged with the cave wall. He climbed up on the boulders, moving stealthily. He balanced on the top boulder, hooking his fingers around the top of the cave, searched for a secure handhold. He would have to do this blindly; he couldn't see out of the cave. He'd have to trust that once he swung himself up and out that he'd be able to slide onto the overhang.

He scanned the stormtroopers, now below him. They were facing forward, blaster rifles held at the ready. No doubt they were waiting for orders on their headsets. Behind the lines the mobile grenade launcher hovered. He saw the stormtrooper on the front platform with his hands on the controls.

Now or never.

He swung out into midair, flipped his body over, missed ramming the cave wall by a hair, and landed on the narrow ledge. He rolled as far back as he could, concealing himself in the shadows. His heart hammered as he waited, wondering whether a grenade would blast him into the sky.

Nothing happened. They hadn't seen him So far, so good.

Ferus felt the Force gather. Garen. Garen had accessed it and it was growing.

Ferus leaped over the heads of the attacking stormtroopers. But if those stormtroopers didn't see him, the ones on the mobile mortar did, clattering it to life. Grenades flew through the air, heading toward him in midair. Garen's lightsaber felt balanced in his hand, and the blue shaft glowed. He deflected the grenades as they whizzed toward him, batting them down to the stormtroopers below.

It felt extraordinary to have a lightsaber back in his hand. His training came back to him, and he didn't have to push for it. It was there in the way he moved, there in the precise angle of his attack.

He landed on the mobile platform, his boots connecting with the stormtrooper and sending him flying off the platform. He slid into the seat, reversed the repulsoriift engine with a jerk, gunning the motor to capacity. The stormtrooper behind fell off.

The battalion scattered before him as he hit them with a barrage of grenades. He could use the mortar to enter the cave and swoop up Garen.

But suddenly the mortar pitched to the side. The

stormtrooper had suddenly leaped back aboard. Ferus felt the heat of a blaster bolt by his ear. He ducked, trying to wield his lightsaber at the same time. It was a difficult move, but one he could have easily managed in his youth. Now his lightsaber skills were rusty and he was just a bit off balance. To Ferus's horror, he began to fall off the mortar as the stormtrooper aimed his blaster and fired.

So. Maybe I'm not as up to speed as I thought I was.

He felt the searing heat in his shoulder. He was blown back off the mortar and hit the ground hard.

Okay. A gorgodon uses me as a punching bag and an evil vision throws me around like a laserball. Now I've been shot with a blaster. Not a good day.

He saw the mortar stop in midair and spin. It was coming back for him.

Fury pounded through him. Fury at himself. He'd blown it. It was going to end here for him, outside the caves of Ilum. The most sacred place to the Jedi, and here his bones would lie. The Force slowed down time, and he reactivated his lightsaber. He couldn't move out of the way of the coming barrage in time, he knew that, but he would join the Force still fighting.

He saw a shimmer out of the corner of his eye, a flicker of light. Something was falling from the sky.

Suddenly, an explosion of light sent him crashing back to the ground.

An alpha charge. A small blast thrown right on the mobile mortar. Then another, and another.

The grenades went up in a huge blast. Ferus rolled down the slope, tumbling, anything to get away from that terrible heat. He came to rest by knocking his head against a boulder.

He saw Trever in a fighter, releasing explosives onto the squad below, with a bulkier transport ship in pursuit. The stormtroopers went scurrying for cover.

Ferus didn't stop to experience the pain he was feeling. He accepted it and set his mind to the next thing. Under the cover of Trever's attack, he took off for the cave. His eyes streamed tears from the smoke, and his shoulder felt as though it was on fire.

He found Garen near the mouth of the cave, slumped on the floor, a blaster held in his fist.

The ship touched down right outside the cave entrance. Ferus picked up Garen. He felt as light as a bird. He ran toward the ramp. The stormtroopers peppered him with blaster bolts, but Trever managed to release a few more explosives behind the boulders, and the blasterfire abated.

Ferus ran up the ramp with Garen. He collapsed on his knees on the floor.

As the transport that had been chasing him made

its way down, Trever jammed the controls up. Pushing the engines, they streaked off. They couldn't boost off-planet, but they could outrun the transport.

"I know a place we can hide," Garen said. "Obi-Wan can find us there."

CHAPTER FIFTEEN

The distress call reached Obi-Wan as he was leaving Polis Massa. He knew exactly which cave they would be hiding in, waiting for him — a crystal-less cave on Ilum that the Jedi often used as a safe hangar.

For the rest of the ride, Obi-Wan could only think two things: *Garen is alive* and *Malorum must be stopped.* When he reached the cave, Ferus and Trever carried Garen on board. Obi-Wan wanted to go back and see his old friend immediately, but he knew a quick escape was essential. It was only after they reached deep space and a recovered Ferus took over the controls that Obi-Wan went back to the cabin to see his friend.

If before he had merely been grateful to know that his friend was alive, now his heart broke to see him.

He would not have recognized him. With his eyes

closed, Garen lay back, his skin as pale and fragile as snow. Obi-Wan felt as though if he breathed on him he could dissolve into vapor. Garen had always been robust and vibrant. His body had crackled with electricity, his eyes brimming with life and humor.

Obi-Wan approached with quiet steps. Garen didn't stir. Obi-Wan could see the delicate blue veins in his eyelids, the dark circles of shadow under his eyes. His cheeks were hollow, his hair sparse. His once muscular chest looked as though it had caved in.

Garen's eyes opened as though it was the hardest thing he ever had to do. He focused on Obi-Wan.

"Can I get you anything?" Obi-Wan asked.

Garen's voice was a whisper. "Just don't bring me a mirror. I can see on your face how bad it is."

"You're alive," Obi-Wan said. "For that I'm thankful."

"I'm not so sure about that, myself. But thanks for finding me."

Each word seemed to cost Garen an effort. What could Obi-Wan do now? How could he care for him? He couldn't bring him back with him to Mos Eisley. It would attract too much attention, and besides, there was hardly good care on Tatooine. He needed rest and constant monitoring.

Garen was already slipping back into unconsciousness.

"We can talk later," Obi-Wan said. He rested a hand on his friend's shoulder, feeling mostly bone. All his feeling welled up in him, the love for his friend, the helplessness he felt, the memory of what Garen had been. The loss of what they'd had.

He collected himself and went back to the cockpit. He slipped into the chair next to Ferus. Trever had given in to exhaustion and had fallen asleep curled up in the galley seating area.

"Thank you for rescuing Garen," Obi-Wan said.

"This is only the beginning," Ferus said. "D'harhan said there was another Jedi prisoner on Coruscant. Garen said he met another Jedi at the cave and she went on to Coruscant. It could be the same Jedi. She could still be alive and a prisoner."

"Coruscant is a big place. She could be anywhere."

"They can't hide a Jedi. We can find her. We can find them all."

"And then what?"

"We take them to a secret base."

Obi-Wan shook his head. "You would only be bringing more danger to them, Ferus. Our best hope for survival is to stay scattered for now. Too much concentrated Force energy in one place might alert the Sith."

"I hardly think a handful of Jedi would trigger a response," Ferus said. "Besides, we'll be well hidden."

"How are you going to find this place?"

"I've already found it. So have you."

Obi-Wan thought for a moment. "The asteroid."

"It's not mapped, it travels constantly."

"It's a hunk of rock with no shelter in the middle of an atmospheric storm."

"See what I mean? Perfect." Ferus's voice was strong, determined. "I've already contacted Roan, my friend from home. I know it was dangerous to risk a transmission, but he's the only person I can trust who isn't already on this ship or on that asteroid. We have a coded system we set up years ago, a series of places to meet. He's bringing supplies and then returning to Ussa. I gave him a detailed list of med supplies that we'll need for Garen and some other things. We'll have to be self-sustaining."

Obi-Wan could hear the excitement in Ferus's voice, but he could not join in. It was not a time to argue. It was a time to rest and plan.

"Wake me when we get to the spaceport," he said.

Trever peered out through the cockpit window at the Nixor spaceport. It was a small port that orbited around the Nixor system. It was a crowded, disorganized mess. The Nixors, feuding with the rest of the system, refused to update the port or even do regular repairs. Pilots went out of their way to avoid it if they could, but it was always crowded due to its central location in the Mid-Rim. It was an easy place to hide.

"You sure pick some nasty holes in the galaxy to meet in," Trever observed.

"That's the whole point. Sometimes the best place to hide is in a crowd." Ferus activated the ramp and hurried down. He searched the scruffy crowd and saw him almost immediately. Roan was thinner, and looked as though he still hadn't fully recovered from his injuries during a stay in an Imperial prison. But his smile was the same.

They walked toward each other slowly.

"You look like a durko on a bad day," Roan said.

Ferus knew it was true. He'd administered bacta on the ship, but the combination of the blaster wound and the battering from the gorgodon had drained him. And given him quite a lovely greenish bruise on his temple, near the silver streak in his hair.

"Thanks. You're not exactly a prize," he answered.

Roan moved forward and grasped Ferus's upper arms. It was their own special greeting to each other after a long absence. When Roan touched Ferus, he saw him grimace.

"What is it?"

"Just a blaster wound. Nothing to worry about."

"Can't you just escape and hide, like everybody else? Do you have to go looking for trouble?" Roan teased, but his eyes were worried.

"Well, you know those Imperials, they're such a bundle of fun. I just can't stay away."

Roan's smile was forced. "I guess you have to do this."

"I do. I wish . . ."

". . . it were different, I know."

"There are Jedi alive out there," Ferus said. "I want to find them, make them safe."

Roan nodded slowly. "I thought you left the Jedi Order."

"I did."

"Really? Doesn't look that way from here."

"Now they need me. Some are still alive. Hiding. If they had a place to come to, a place to be safe, that would give them a chance to fight again. So I'm going to establish a secret base."

"Ah, that explains the greenhouse," Roan said.

"Were you able to bring it?"

"I have a pre-fab greenhouse, food supplies, seeds, plants, water purifying system, and a complete med unit. Everything you asked for. Plus extra fuel and some datapads, a few other things. Your vioflute, so you can torture others in the evenings the way you used to torture me."

Ferus laughed, but sadness overtook him. His old life was truly gone. Gone forever.

"You're putting yourself in great danger," Roan said. "But I guess you know that. Well, don't worry, partner. We can see each other from time to time. I have work to do on Ussa, too. The Empire has cracked down on the resistance, but we're biding our time. You're doing the right thing."

"I don't know if that's true," Ferus said. "I only know I have to do it."

"Sometimes," Roan said, "that's all you get to know."

CHAPTER SIXTEEN

The homing beacon worked perfectly, but they still had to dive into the atmospheric storm to make it back to the asteroid. Ferus was more used to the space shears now as well as the sudden gravity vortexes that could send the ship spinning out of control. Still, when the asteroid came into view, they all breathed a sigh of relief.

Toma and Raina must have seen them approach, because they stood waiting while Ferus landed the craft. Ferus lowered the ramp and the three of them walked down.

"We're very glad to see you," Toma said.

"We were getting tired of each other's conversation," Raina said. She was trying to joke, but there was strain on her face. No doubt she'd been afraid they weren't going to return.

"We have supplies," Ferus said. "And a wounded comrade."

"Let me see to him," Raina said. "Before the Clone Wars, I was completing my med training." She lightly ran up the ramp into the ship.

Ferus turned back to Toma. "We are going to establish a base here. We hope to find more Jedi to come. I have enough supplies to keep us self-sustaining. What I need is for beings to run it while I'm away. I was hoping to talk you and Raina into it. I realize it's not exactly an appealing job, but . . ."

"I can't speak for Raina," Toma said, "but I can imagine no better cause."

They unloaded the supplies. Obi-Wan and Ferus and Toma set up the prefabricated housing that was packed neatly into durasteel containers. The plastoid structures were durable and built to withstand heat and cold.

When they were done, they paused to watch the dark sky overhead. Since the asteroid traveled continuously and had no sun, it did not have a division between night and day. Still, there was the feeling that a day had passed, and it was time for sleep.

Obi-Wan looked in on Garen. Raina had set up a kind of clinic in one of the structures. Garen was sleeping.

"It will take some time for him to recover," Raina said quietly. "There is nothing we can't do for him here that he couldn't get in a first-class facility. He needs rest and food and basic med care. I'll make him better, Obi-Wan." She looked at Garen with sorrow in her face. "I remember him from the Clone Wars. He's greatly changed."

He put his hand on her shoulder. "Thank you for caring for him."

Obi-Wan ducked out of the structure. Ferus was standing alone, looking up at the sky.

"How's Garen?"

"Sleeping. Raina doesn't know how long his recovery will take. But he'll be all right here."

"Now that he's settled, I think we should leave for Coruscant," Ferus said. "We've no time to lose."

Here it was. Here was the moment he would disappoint him. "I'm not coming with you, Ferus."

Ferus looked saddened, but not surprised. "I guess I knew that. I just hoped you'd change your mind."

"I have given you as much help as I can give."

"What about Garen? He's your friend!"

"I'm leaving him in a place he can be cared for."

"Yes, he needs care. That's my point. We found Garen, and we know there is another Jedi who needs our help." Ferus shook his head. "I don't understand how you can walk away from that."

"And I can't explain." *There are some things you just can't know.*

Ferus snorted. "Your secret mission again."

"I'm sorry I can't tell you. If you need my help from time to time, I'll help you. But I can't build this base for you. I can't travel the galaxy with you. I have my place in this struggle already mapped out."

He could see the impatience on Ferus's face. "So you'll abandon the ones who need you, like your best friend?"

"They have you. This is your mission, Ferus. You chose it."

Ferus looked away, furious.

Obi-Wan's own feelings were a tangle inside him. He couldn't say that he didn't think Ferus had a point. Part of him wondered if he was abandoning Garen, and he worried about this fragile group. Toma and Raina were courageous and resourceful, but they could only do so much. Trever was sharp and inventive, but he was still a boy. Garen was ill and frail. And Ferus was just putting his feet back on the path. He took on too much, thinking he was still as powerful a Jedi as he used to be.

And he was leaving all of them to fend for themselves.

He was doing the right thing. He knew that. But to go on, to do that thing, to not have regrets . . . that was something he wasn't capable of.

Acceptance doesn't guard you from regret.

It was a memory this time, and it rang clear as

a bell in Obi-Wan's mind. He and Qui-Gon having one of their many talks after a mission. He couldn't remember now what it was that he regretted, or what he had been asking. But he remembered a blazing sunset and the beginnings of the night sky above it, and he clearly remembered Qui-Gon's answer.

To be a living being is to live with regret. Those who say they regret nothing are liars or fools. Accept your regret the way you accept your mistakes. Then move on.

Obi-Wan looked at Ferus, and he felt pain in his heart. Ferus was so brave, and there was so much ahead of him. Yet he must leave him. The fact that his heart could break, the fact that he could be filled with this confusion . . . that was something he hadn't felt in a long while. It was something he'd hoped never to feel again. Yet here he was, his heart full of feeling.

And then he knew, as surely as he knew his mission, why Qui-Gon had told him he wasn't ready for training with the Whills.

When you know why you are not ready, you will be ready, Qui-Gon had told him.

Now he knew. Now he was ready to return.

"I have two things to ask of you," Obi-Wan said. "One is Garen."

"I will see that he's cared for," Ferus said stiffly. "You don't have to ask. I'll never abandon him."

"Thank you. Now I must ask you something else. I'm afraid that Malorum is looking into Polis Massa. It's best if you don't know why. I managed to deflect the inquiry for a time, but I don't know what Malorum knows or what he's planning to do next. The answers to those questions can endanger every Jedi — and the fledgling resistance."

"I'll track him for you," Ferus said. "It may take some time."

"Do your best," Obi-Wan said. "If he continues to investigate, I'll need to know. On your way to Coruscant, I need you to drop me on Tatooine. It's time for me to get back."

"You're treating me like an apprentice," Ferus said. "You won't tell me what you're doing, and you're giving me orders."

"It seems that way," Obi-Wan said. "But I don't think of you as an apprentice."

"What do you think of me as, then?" Ferus asked irritably.

"A Jedi," Obi-Wan said. "One of the last."

Ferus's troubled gaze cleared. He took a deep breath that seemed to calm him.

"It's been so long since I was a Jedi," he said. "The old ways are ingrained in me, but I have to struggle to rediscover them. Acceptance, right? Acceptance without judgment. That's what I need."

"It's something to strive for, anyway."

Ferus turned to face him. Obi-Wan saw that Ferus didn't understand him. Hadn't forgiven him. But he had taken a step on the path. "Then I will try."

CHAPTER SEVENTEEN

They landed Toma's ship outside the settlement of Mos Eisley. Obi-Wan wrapped his cloak around him. The wind was up, and the sand outside was blowing crazily. Good. Everyone tended to stay in their shelters during sandstorms. He would have a solitary walk to his dwelling.

"Good-bye, Trever," Obi-Wan said. "We've had an interesting journey together. May the Force be with you."

"Back at you, 'Wan."

Trever went back into the ship, and Obi-Wan stood at the top of the ramp with Ferus. Particles of sand stung their cheeks and exposed skin.

"Charming place," Ferus remarked. "I can see why you want to stay."

"And your asteroid is a garden?"

"Ah, but it will be."

Obi-Wan paused. There was a part of him that wanted to stay with Ferus, to hold on to this one human link to the past. But he knew what he had to do, and that he had to do it alone.

"I'm glad our paths crossed again," he said now.

"You were kind to me as an apprentice," Ferus replied. "I admired you more than any Jedi . . . you and Siri. Now I guess I have to trust you, too. That's not as easy."

"Qui-Gon would say that when it comes to the Living Force, trust is the only currency," Obi-Wan said.

Ferus nodded. "You said you would help me if I needed it. I pledge the same to you. May the Force be with you, Obi-Wan Kenobi."

"May the Force be with you," Obi-Wan said. "Find them and gather them. Make them safe."

With his hand on his new lightsaber, Ferus strode back up the ramp. Obi-Wan stepped back onto the rocky soil of Tatooine. He retreated to the relative shelter of a cliff overhang to watch as Ferus did a flight check before departure.

A voice entered his head.

I never said trust was the currency of the Living Force. This time, Qui-Gon sounded dry, amused.

Obi-Wan smiled. "You didn't?"

I don't think I'd say anything that pompous. It sounds more like you.

Obi-Wan leaned against the rock wall. "It's good to be back."

Something has changed with you. I sense it.

"I know now why I wasn't ready to receive the training," Obi-Wan said. "I had lost my connection to the Living Force. You taught me, my life had taught me, Siri taught me . . . how to connect to the Living Force. I learned to live with an open heart. But then Anakin turned to the dark side, and I lost my perspective."

You felt only rage and blame and you turned it on yourself.

"There was much to blame myself for."

Maybe.

"But still, I couldn't see my way out of it."

You bore all the responsibility for what happened. You went over and over your mistakes. You must know this, Obi-Wan — it is Anakin who chose to turn to the dark side. Grief did not push him there. You did not push him there. He made the choice.

"There were so many things I should have seen. So many places I should have corrected him."

Yes. But you must accept your regret the way you accept your mistakes. Then move on.

"Someone told me that once, long ago."

The smile had come back into Qui-Gon's voice. *Pity you didn't listen.*

Obi-Wan felt something lift. Qui-Gon was right. Blame was crippling him, and now it was gone.

He had learned to forgive himself. He had learned to open himself up to pain again.

He was no longer the same man he was when he first exiled himself on Tatooine. He had wanted to exile more than himself. He had wanted to exile his heart.

Well, he would live here, and he would watch over Luke, but he wouldn't stop living.

And he would start with forgiveness for his mistakes. He knew now that he was part of one great struggle. The galaxy did not turn on his failures. It did not rest on his success.

The power of the Empire was awesome. Fearsome. But Luke and Leia were alive. Ferus was alive, and maybe other Jedi were, too. Someday, a rebellion would rise.

Obi-Wan watched the gray ship lift into the air and disappear from sight. Ferus was the future. Ferus would take up the fight that Obi-Wan could not join.

Obi-Wan readied his mind. He felt Qui-Gon's presence, steady and sure.

"I am ready to begin," he said.

CHAPTER EIGHTEEN

Ferus eased the ship into the crowded express space lane toward the surface of Coruscant. Trever had never seen so much space traffic. The lanes were dense with vehicles, all jockeying for position.

"Never seen anything like it, right?" Ferus asked.

"Never."

"It has just about anything you'd want," Ferus said, waving a hand at the thousands of buildings. Trever felt awed. He'd never seen so many lights, and behind every light was a business, a home, a dwelling. "And I have contacts here. It might be a place for you to put down roots."

An ache twisted Trever's stomach. He'd thought he and Ferus were partners. Sure, he'd thought about leaving him on Ilum, but he hadn't. Now Ferus was taking the first occasion to dump him.

Ferus saw the look on his face. "What is it?"

Trever's face hardened. "Ready to unload the space garbage, huh?"

"No," Ferus said. "But I have a new goal now. It's dangerous. I don't know where I'll be going, how I'll be living. I can't drag you into that."

"You're not dragging me."

"And you can't tell me that you haven't thought of leaving," Ferus said. "There are easier ways to live."

"Okay, I've thought about it," Trever admitted. "And I can't say I'm crazy about this Jedi-base business. But I don't know, I feel kind of stuck with you. That's the awful, new-moon truth."

Ferus laughed. "Thanks. I guess."

Trever stretched out and propped his feet on the console. "So if you don't mind, I'm not going anywhere just yet."

Ferus knew he should keep a low profile. He knew he should dock at the most crowded spaceport and lose himself in the vast crowds.

But he couldn't resist passing the Jedi Temple. He had to see.

It rose before him. At first, it seemed a mirage, unreal, a holo-projection. Because this couldn't be real.

The towers — broken. The top half of the Temple spires — scorched by fire.

It was ruined. The gracious rooms, the hallways, the gardens, the fountains.

Gone.

A deep tremor went through him. His hands shook on the controls. Beside him, even Trever was silent.

Had he really absorbed the loss of the Jedi until this moment? It didn't seem so. Now it filled him up. He choked on his rage, on his pain. On his sorrow.

They would be in danger on Coruscant every moment. He didn't know where to start looking for the imprisoned Jedi. He didn't know which of his old contacts were dead. Some could now be spies for the Empire. He was in a new galaxy now, and he wasn't sure he had the tools to maneuver through it.

But with his eyes on the devastation of the Temple, he was more certain than ever of his path.

Why him? The visions had accused him of arrogance. But Ferus knew the answer was simple. He was the only one who could. He would find the last of the Jedi and bring them home.